The Enemy Within

(Joseph #2)

*Note: *The Enemy Within* is written as a sequel. While it can be read as a stand-alone book, the story will seem more complete if you first read *Do No Harm*.*

Also by Danielle Singleton:

Safe & Sound
Do No Harm (Joseph #1)
The Containment Zone
Price of Life

Connect with the author online:

www.daniellesingleton.com
@auntdanwrites
www.facebook.com/singletondanielle
www.daniellesingleton.wordpress.com

The Enemy Within

Danielle Singleton

ISBN: 1491241470

*****

To Gus:
For Your Unconditional Love

"Outside of a dog, a book is a man's best
friend. Inside of a dog it's too dark to read."

Groucho Marx

ACKNOWLEDGMENTS

All praise and glory to my Lord and Savior Jesus Christ. I am eternally grateful. (See what I did there?)

Thank you again to my incredible Reading Committee. Y'all help make my books what they are, and I deeply appreciate your feedback and suggestions. A particular thank you to my sister for suggesting that I write a sequel to *Do No Harm*, and to Jamie McGinnis and John O'Keefe for their character name ideas. Also a special thanks to William Allen and Allen Hartley - the combined inspirations for Agent Allen Williams.

I also want to acknowledge David Singleton for all of his publicity help. "U R great. Aw right!"

Many thanks to Greg Stephenson and Jonnie Moeller of the Marietta Police Department for helping with the book research. Y'all certainly helped the characters come to life!

And even though he also got the Dedication, I would be remiss if I didn't mention the big brown dog. My biggest fan (the feeling is mutual).

I hope y'all enjoy the story.

The Enemy Within

*****

"There was never a genius without a tincture
of madness."

Aristotle

ONE

Joseph knew the exact moment when Reagan White found out that he was responsible for the biological attacks. She tried to hide it, and did a fairly good job, but not good enough.

He saw the flash of confusion, followed quickly by fear, as she read the text message on her phone. And he saw it in her eyes when she looked back up at him. Two blue-green pools of panic. *Much to Agent White's credit*, thought Joseph, *her voice wasn't noticeably different. Although I did catch her off guard by wishing her well at the end of our conversation.* He chuckled. *Stupid woman.*

Joseph's happy mood didn't last long, though. He knew he had to hurry. Grabbing his car keys from the side pocket of his briefcase, Joseph ran over to his office door and looked around the corner, just in time to catch a glimpse of Agent White as she turned to walk down the hall housing the elevators.

Whereas Reagan had gone right, Joseph went left, bolting down the hall at a full sprint and crashing through the door that led to the stairwell. Taking the concrete steps two at a time, Joseph quickly reached the first floor of his office building. He then continued his mad dash, going out the side exit and making a beeline for his car.

Joseph was breathing heavily by the time he sat down in the driver's seat and cranked up his trusty silver sedan. "Fuck," he exclaimed in between breaths, "I'm out of shape."

It was in that moment that Joseph saw the object of his attention exiting the front doors of the National Institutes of Health. Shifting his car into gear, Joseph's tires squealed as he slammed in his foot down on the gas pedal and took off. Directly in his sights was Agent Reagan White.

****

Two years earlier . . .

A funny thing happens when a person gets away with murder: he starts to think he can get away with it again. Dr. Joseph Isaac Carlson wasn't just a run of the mill murderer, either. He had thirty-one dead bodies to his name. Or, rather, thirty-one dead bodies *not* to his name.

A year earlier, Joseph had gotten frustrated by what he viewed as a lack of respect for his genius and his work. So he designed and delivered a virus into America's blood supply that had a kill rate of one hundred percent. Every single infected person died. *Perfection*, the doctor thought. *Perfect virus, perfect murder percentage, and perfect escape.* Part of the pathologist's master plan was that he led the medical team tasked with defeating the virus he created. When the group of six doctors finally created a test to screen blood for the virus, Joseph managed to convince everyone that the outbreaks simply were caused by a random, short-lived genetic mutation. *Game over.* Dr. Carlson and his team were honored at the White House for their service to the country, people were no longer afraid to receive blood transfusions, and all was well in the world of Joseph.

But now, one year later, things weren't quite so good. Joseph still received research projects from both the government and outside pharmaceutical companies, he was still invited to speak at countless medical symposia, and, most importantly, he was still considered to be the best pathologist in the country. Despite all of that, the forty-six year old bachelor wasn't happy. And the reason was simple: he missed killing people.

Joseph Isaac Carlson didn't kill anyone until he reached his mid-forties. In fact, as a doctor, he did just the opposite. He saved lives. But the millionaire infectious disease expert had quickly discovered during 'Operation Respect' that the high that came from saving a life was nowhere near the rush of taking one.

His first murders had been utilitarian in nature: he needed the homeless people's blood for his virus. Joseph also had to kill the little girl from his neighborhood, Peyton Finch, in order to keep his domestic terrorism plot a secret. And the people who died after being infected with his virus - nicknamed SuperAIDS - were just collateral damage.

All of those murders - thirty-one in total - were simply the means to an end. Nevertheless, a funny thing happened while Joseph was killing his victims . . . he started to like it. He got hooked.

****

Much like any other junkie, Joseph found himself looking for his next 'high'. But any regular old murder wouldn't do. Even though Carlson wanted to start killing again, he wasn't going to start knocking off random people just for the heck of it. Joseph had a world class mind, and he needed a world class challenge.

"I could always do another round with something medical," he said aloud. Dr. Carlson was sitting at his kitchen table eating a quick breakfast before heading off to work at the National Institutes of Health in Bethesda, Maryland. Joseph was Chief of Pathology at the NIH and in charge of one of the United States' most sophisticated biomedical research labs.

"But it couldn't actually be a virus," he reasoned. "That would be too obvious." The doctor's words echoed around his kitchen and through his empty house. Joseph's last visitor had been over a year ago, and she left wrapped in a plastic tarp.

"We need something good," concluded Dr. Carlson, falling into his habit of speaking with the royal we.

"Something different, something deadly . . . something worth my time."

The doctor's thoughts were preoccupied for the next several days while he tried to think of the perfect disease to use in his new killing scheme. The last one was a specially-engineered blood-borne virus with symptoms mimicking AIDS and patient death within a month of infection. SuperAIDS was the vehicle behind Operation Respect, but Joseph now had the respect he wanted. *That's not the issue anymore*, he thought as he fiddled with a slide on the microscope in front of him in his lab at work. *Operation Death? No, that's too corny.* Joseph spun around on his stool and stood up. *Maybe I don't need it to have a name*, he concluded. *I do need to figure out how I'm going to kill the people, though.*

TWO

A few weeks later, Dr. Carlson sat as his desk and drummed his fingers against his coffee cup, still stewing over how he could start another round of murders. His weapon of choice this time couldn't be a virus; he knew that. Even though his National Institutes of Health team had officially labeled his first virus a 'spontaneous mutation,' Joseph didn't want anyone to pick up on any similarities.

An article in the National Journal of Pathology was what finally gave Carlson the inspiration he needed to create his new deadly illness. The magazine was talking about advances in prosthetics and the challenges that doctors faced when trying to fit artificial limbs onto victims of flesh-eating bacteria.

Joseph couldn't care less about the prosthetics, but he was very interested in the illness mentioned. *Flesh eating bacteria*, he thought. *Yeah . . . that just might work.*

Dr. Carlson's second-in-command, Keri Dupree, walked into the room and broke Joseph's train of thought.

"Hey Isaac," the brunette said, calling him by the name he had always used professionally. "I just wanted to let you know that I'm going to have to leave early this afternoon."

Carlson rolled his eyes but didn't issue any comment in return. Keri used to work the kind of hours he expected of a top research physician . . . not the same amount of time that he did, but nobody worked as long or as hard as Isaac Carlson.

Keri used to work long hours, but that was B.M. - before Matty. Dr. Dupree's four month old little bundle of screaming, pooping misery had completely taken over her and her husband's lives. And Dr. Carlson had lost his best lab assistant in the process.

"Did you hear me?" Keri asked.

"What? Yeah, I heard you. Leaving early. Again."

This time it was Keri's turn to roll her eyes. "Don't give me that." Motherhood had taught the thirty-six year old many things, one of which was how to better stand up to her boss. "I put in a full work week, every week, and you know it," the feisty woman continued. "In fact, I knew I would be leaving early today so I worked extra hours earlier this week."

Dr. Carlson sighed. "Whatever."

"Don't you want to know where I'm going?" Keri asked. She knew her boss well enough to know that he didn't care, but she was so excited about her afternoon mission that she was going to tell him about it anyway.

"Not really," the man grumbled in response.

Ignoring him, Keri went on: "I'm going to this little boutique shop in Georgetown," she beamed. "They have the cutest stuff for little boys for Father's Day."

Isaac responded by turning away and looking down through the lens of his microscope, but Keri was undeterred.

"It's Scott's first year getting to celebrate Father's Day as a dad, and I want to make sure it's really special. He's so excited - everyone at his firm is probably getting annoyed by how much he talks about the baby."

"I know how they feel."

"Well, too bad," Dr. Dupree replied. "I got used to having people around to talk to during the SuperAIDS case, and I liked it. There's no reason why we can't talk while we work."

"Yes there is," Isaac said.

"What?"

"I don't want to."

Keri couldn't help but laugh a little bit at Dr. Carlson's grumpy attitude. "Oh come on, you must have some fond memories of Father's Day from when you were a kid."

"Nope."

"None? I find that hard to believe. You and your dad didn't go camping or play golf or anything?"

"No," Isaac replied, slamming his hands down on the table in front of him. "Now drop it."

Keri knew from her boss' tone that he was no longer just his usual grumpy; now he was mad. Deciding it was best to just leave him alone, Keri issued a curt "fine" before turning around and walking back out of his office.

****

Keri was right: Joseph was mad. His parents, and *especially* his father, were not suitable topics of conversation. Ever. Mother's and Father's Day were not celebrated in his home as a child, and they sure as hell wouldn't be celebrated in his lab as an adult.

Joseph Carlson, Jr. remembered the time when he was in kindergarten and everyone in his class made paper plate gifts for Mother's Day. The pale-faced, spectacled little Joey had been so proud of his artwork. So proud, in fact, that he built up enough courage to knock on the door to Joseph Sr.'s study and show his dad the gift for his mom.

The elder Carlson was visibly irritated by his young son's intrusion, but the boy hadn't been old enough to pick up on that. So he walked straight up to his father's desk, grinning from ear to ear with his baby-toothed smile.

"Look, Dad!" little Joseph had declared, proudly placing the pink-and-white colored paper plate on the desk with its 'Happy Mother's Day' message spelled out in glitter.

"What the hell is that?" his father grumbled, the same grumble with which Keri was now so familiar.

"It's a present for Mom," Joseph Jr. answered, undeterred. "For Mother's Day."

"You are not giving that to your mother."

His father's stern rejection confused the five-year-old. "Why not?"

"Your mother does not want a shitty paper plate that will just spill glitter everywhere. Now leave," the surgeon said, dismissing his namesake with a wave of his hand. "I have work to do."

It was less than a year later when the young Joseph Carlson got his first full glimpse of how his parents felt about him. The boy's nanny had put in her notice two months earlier, making sure to give Dr. and Mrs. Carlson ample time to find her replacement. Lillian Carlson had assured the former nanny, a nice woman who was only leaving because she was getting married, that the family had taken care of things regarding a new caretaker for the boy. And Joseph's mom had intended to, but then things just got so busy with her social calendar that it slipped her mind.

That was how it came to pass that the first-grader found himself sitting in the front office of his private school well after the time when someone should have come to pick him up. The old nanny's last day was the previous Friday, and no new nanny had been hired.

Joseph shuddered at his desk while remembering how his skinny six year old self sat on the edge of a plastic chair, swallowed up by the oversized backpack that he refused to take off his shoulders. Joseph Jr. knew the adults in the room were looking at him, talking about him, but he had just continued to stare at the floor and stub his tennis-shoed toes into the carpet.

"I can't get hold of either of his parents," one office worker had whispered loudly enough that Joseph could hear her. "The hospital said that his dad is in surgery and no one answered their home phone."

A second woman sighed and shook her head, glancing over at the little boy with a look of pity on her face. "I don't even know why they had him in the first place. His nanny is the only one who ever spends any time with him."

The first lady, the one who tried contacting Joseph's parents, nodded her head in agreement. After twelve years of working at Seattle's most prestigious grammar school, she wasn't surprised by the Carlson's behavior. "You know how it is with these types. They don't want to have kids. They just want a little person who the nanny can bring out to display for their friends. This kid is a decoration in his house, nothing else."

The final nail in the coffin of Joseph's relationship with his parents was his medical school graduation. It hurt the doctor to think about it even now, a full twenty years later. The young man was graduating with highest honors, having earned both his medical degree and a Masters in Public Health from Harvard University. But on that late May morning, when Cambridge, Massachusetts was overflowing with graduates, friends, and relatives from all over the world, Dr. and Mrs. Joseph Carlson Sr. were nowhere to be found. The elder doctor's parents, Joseph's grandparents, were in attendance and visibly ecstatic about their grandson's big day. But the graduate's father had knowingly scheduled a surgery for every day that week, and Lillian Carlson preferred to sit in the gallery and watch her husband work. Neither gave any thought to attending their son's graduation. Neither cared at all about the award he would receive for having the highest grade point average in his class, or the special recognition he earned for being the only Class of 1993 graduate to have already published an article in the National Journal of Medicine.

It was in that moment, walking across the stage and looking out in the crowd to see that none of the smiling faces belonged to his parents, that Joseph I. Carlson became J. Isaac Carlson. The son wanted absolutely nothing to do with the father. He even considered switching his last name from Carlson to his mother's maiden name, but *Isaac* had been made fun of enough as a child and didn't want to give anyone fodder for more with the unfortunate name Butts.

By the time the erstwhile aspiring surgeon exited the stage with his diploma in hand, the conversion was complete. Isaac was chosen over Joseph. Pathology over surgery. East Coast over West. The young man's grandparents could already see a difference in him when they met up on Harvard's famed green lawn to celebrate.

"Congratulations darling!" June Carlson had exclaimed, enveloping her only grandchild in a bear hug. "We're so proud of you!"

Bo Carlson nodded his head. "Well done, Joey. This is quite an accomplishment."

"Thanks," the young man replied. "And actually, I've decided that I'm going to go by Isaac from now on. I want to build my own reputation as a doctor and not be known as Joseph Jr." The newly minted doctor then pointedly looked around to make a show of the absence of his parents.

"I'm sorry they aren't here, baby," his grandmother said. "But we are, we love you, and we're so very, very proud. And you definitely look like an Isaac to me."

Dr. Carlson had smiled and hugged the older woman. His parents were never affectionate with him and showing any emotion - even with his grandmother - made Joseph feel uncomfortable. But he knew the hug pleased Grandma June and he wanted to do something to return the only true love ever shown to him.

His grandfather, the soft-spoken son of a farmer, had always been a man of few words. As such, Grandpa Carlson's next statement on graduation day had stuck with his grandson throughout the following decades.

"I fought against enemies foreign in the Second World War," the old man said. "And then I came home and fought enemies domestic as a police officer. But you, my boy, will face a different kind of enemy. It's foreign because it doesn't belong, but it's domestic because it's within us. But what's important, Jos - *Isaac*, is that you face it. You fight it. You don't run from it. You stick with it, and, eventually, you'll beat it."

The young man had nodded his head in agreement. "I will, Grandpa."

****

Twenty years later, Dr. Carlson leaned back in his chair and ran his hands through his almost completely gray hair. In that moment, Joseph realized exactly how prescient his grandfather's words had been. *The enemy is within*, he thought. *It's within me.*

Isaac was the persona and the name that Dr. Carlson had used ever since his graduation from Harvard. While 'nice' wouldn't exactly be the word people would use to describe Isaac Carlson, he received solid marks as professionally courteous. Kind to his patients. Dedicated. Persistent. All good traits. Positive traits. Isaac traits.

When he decided to start Operation Respect, though, Joseph had returned. Harsh. Cruel. Brilliant, yet unfeeling. It helped Dr. Carlson to think in terms of Joseph when working on his secret killer projects. Joseph was like his father, in name and in attitude. Joseph killed people and didn't care. And if the NIH pathologist could have found a way to include Joseph Sr. on his hit list, he would've.

"The enemy is within," he repeated. "And I like it that way."

THREE

With Father's Day past him and the heat of a mid-Atlantic summer descending on the Washington, DC suburbs, Dr. Carlson found himself spending more and more time in the basement laboratory in his house - both for his secret project and the room's naturally cooler temperatures. Even though he already decided to use a flesh-eating bacteria, Joseph was still brainstorming ways to expose people to his new killer disease. The blood supply was out as an option . . . he couldn't repeat anything from his previous round of murders.

I could dump it in lakes or ponds where people swim, Joseph thought. *Although, I don't think that would give us the kind of full exposure we need. I don't want amputated limbs. I want dead bodies.*

Dr. Carlson drummed his fingers on his metal worktable. "Come on Joe . . . think."

****

The idea Joseph was searching for came to him several days later while he was watching the news. A story was being run about a water treatment plant in a small town in rural Georgia that had been broken into by vandals. Officials said that the perpetrators altered the filtration settings and that a boil water alert was issued for everyone in the area. The newscaster then went on to editorialize about how counterterrorism experts worried about potential attacks on America's water supply since so many treatment plants were secured by only flimsy gates or padlocked chains.

"That's brilliant," Joseph said aloud. "Absolutely brilliant. If I can get the bacteria into the water supply and get people to drink it, it'll wreak havoc on their bodies before the doctors know what hit them." Dr. Carlson grinned. "This is going to be great."

Joseph stood up from his couch and walked toward his kitchen island. The door to his basement laboratory was hidden on the end of the island's cabinets, and he wanted to get in some work that night after having finally figured out his plan of attack.

A few steps from the counter, he stopped. "How the hell," Joseph asked aloud, "am I going to do what I need to do to make this bacteria without the feds tapping me as a terrorist?" Dr. Carlson sighed. This hadn't been as much of a problem two years earlier when he created his blood-borne virus. *Or maybe it was*, he thought, *and I just wasn't aware of it.* Public knowledge of the government's snooping abilities had grown greatly since the last time Joseph wanted to research ways to kill people.

"I need something old school," he said. "No record. No history. Never leave a trail."

****

Eventually the pathologist settled on the library at the University of Maryland Medical School in nearby Baltimore. He drove up there after work one day, flashed his NIH badge at the entrance, and made his way through the tall stacks of books in the infectious diseases section. *Where is everybody?* Joseph thought. *Students should be here studying.*

A second later, Dr. Carlson realized why he was alone in the research room. "They're all doing work on the internet. Nobody uses real books anymore." He laughed. "Fine by me . . . fewer people around to bother me or see what I'm doing."

Joseph spent each night for the next several weeks at the university library, looking up everything from which kinds of bacteria can cause flesh eating symptoms to how each of those bacteria would respond to a variety of antibiotics.

Carlson studied flesh-eating bacteria, or necrotizing fasciitis, very briefly in medical school, but it was more of 'hey look isn't this cool' than 'let's seriously learn about this disease.' During Operation Respect, Joseph would look up something, test it in his lab, and then adjust his research based on the laboratory outcomes. But under these circumstances, Dr. Carlson wanted to explore all possibilities and have them at hand in his notebook. *I can't keep coming back up here every other night while I'm running tests in my lab*, he thought.

Night after night and on weekends as well, the renowned pathologist scribbled more and more information into his research notebook. *It doesn't matter that the disease affects people more if they have weakened immune systems*, he reasoned, *since I won't have any way of controlling who is infected.* Then: *small towns will probably be better than cities because the symptoms are rare and confusing and rural hospitals are less likely to have higher-end antibiotics.*

Point after point, page after page, Joseph plotted his course of action with the bacteria. "It can't just be another strand of necrotizing fasciitis," he whispered to himself in the library. "It needs to be like the SuperAIDS virus . . . I need it to walk like this disease and talk like this disease but not actually be this disease."

When the medical part of Carlson's research was finished, he changed locations from Baltimore to College Park so he could work at the University of Maryland's science library. "I might be able to feel my way through the bacteria stuff, but I don't have a clue about water treatment plants."

Wanting to have a complete understanding of the process, Dr. Carlson began at the beginning and learned the history of drinking water filtration. About how in 1804 Paisley, Scotland was the first town to receive filtered water, and how they used a slow sand filter - a biological process that uses a gelatinous film growing on the top of the sand to clean the water. He then progressed to learning about the rapid sand filter, a combination of chemicals and granular elements that removes impurities from the water. Joseph quickly graduated to screens, pH adjustments, flocculation, and a whole host of other chemistry terms that told him everything he needed to know to make his deadly bacteria.

So, in a nutshell, he thought, *anything and everything that can filter out unwanted particles or chemically bind to dangerous elements in water is used in order to make the water as clean as possible.* Joseph was actually quite relieved to learn how extensive the modern water cleaning process was. The big plants that he would be targeting didn't just run the water through one round of cleaning; it went through multiple levels of filtration before reaching anyone's home.

That makes me feel better about my drinking water, for sure, but it also makes this project more difficult, he concluded. My bacteria *needs to be microscopic,* he thought, *so that it won't get caught in any of the screen filters they have. But it also needs to be of an entirely new composition so that the treatment chemicals and coagulates won't kill it.* He scribbled more information in his notepad before closing the chemistry textbook in front of him.

"Time to change gears," Joseph said aloud. On this particular October Saturday afternoon, the library was almost empty given the football game on campus later that night. While the past several weeks had been spent learning about the drinking water filtration process, Dr. Carlson knew he now needed to focus on treatment plants that were already completed. More accurately, he needed to pick out the locations where he would make his biological attacks. *I don't want to do anything on the internet since the police can track that, but I really don't have any choice in the matter,* he thought. *There's no other way to find out what I need to know.*

Joseph rose from the table where he had been reading chemistry textbooks and walked over to the librarian's helpdesk. "Excuse me?"

"Yes, hi," a plump elderly woman said. "How can I help you?"

"I'd like to use one of the computers for some research but there was a note on the screen saying I needed an access card."

The librarian looked at Joseph skeptically. "Are you a student here?"

"No. I'm an adjunct professor," he replied. Which was true . . . kind of. Ever since his heroics in the SuperAIDS case, Joseph had been a guest lecturer at the medical school numerous times.

Dr. Carlson's answer appeared to appease the librarian. "Okay," she said, handing him a clipboard with a form attached. "I'll need you to fill this out first. It just says who you are so we can make sure the general public isn't coming in to use our facilities."

Without thinking about it, Joseph scribbled down his name and NIH contact information on the form before returning it to the lady seated behind the desk in front of him.

"Wonderful, thank you," she said. "Here's your access card. Just swipe it through the black box next to the computer you're using and it'll let you get on the internet."

Well that was a pain in the butt, Joseph thought as he walked to the computer lab in the library. *But now the cops won't be able to see what I'm researching on the internet. If I had done this search at home, it would show up in my browser history. But not here.* The doctor smiled. *Never leave a trail.*

Three hours and dozens of websites later, Carlson had compiled a full list of possible drop locations. Forty-five places in total, spread throughout the country. Leaning back in his chair, the evil doctor took off his glasses and rubbed his tired eyes. It had taken longer than he wanted - a month and a half of nights and weekends to be exact - but Joseph had finally reached the point where he felt comfortable in his knowledge of how to create and enact his new deadly scheme. "I think I've got it," Dr. Carlson declared. "Well, I've got the idea for it," he corrected himself. "Now let's see if we can get it in the lab, too."

FOUR

Six months passed before Joseph made any significant progress on his flesh-eating bacteria. The longest amount of time was spent building his own water filtration machines. Dr. Carlson was a brilliant physician and medical researcher, but carpenter and engineer he was not. With that finally out of the way, Joseph was able to settle down and begin working on his bacteria.

Dr. Carlson needed to keep up his usual work routine, which included fourteen-hour workdays and usually an appearance or two each weekend at his National Institutes of Health office. Every other waking hour, though, and many times hours during which he should have been asleep, Joseph tinkered away in his secret home lab. He occasionally wondered if the way he planned his attacks was the same way all terrorists planned theirs. The doctor had long ago gotten over any stigma that he might have felt at labeling himself a terrorist. Now, instead, smack in the middle of his second orchestrated mass murdering, he embraced it. The yellow 'don't tread on me' flag adorning the otherwise bare walls of his underground workspace was proof thereof. "After all," Joseph said to himself, "what was George Washington if not the leader of a terrorist organization? One man's terrorist is another man's freedom fighter," he added with conviction.

Joseph checked his watch. *Three am.* He stood up from his desk and stretched.

I should probably call it a night. A second later, the doctor sat back down. *No, Joe, keep going.* "This research is already taking long enough," he said with a sigh. "Getting this thing done will take sacrifice. Winning takes sacrifice." Joseph picked up the petri dish he had set down a few minutes earlier. "I want to win." He grinned. "People don't like it when the bad guy wins."

Dr. Carlson's grin turned into laughter, its evil sound echoing off the concrete walls. "Good thing I don't care what people think."

The world-renowned pathologist was lying - he absolutely did care what people thought - but there wasn't anyone else in his house to call him on his fibs. The only other living creatures who ever occupied Joseph's suburban home were the little white mice he used for lab tests. And right then there weren't even any of those scurrying around.

"Which reminds me," Joseph said. "I need to pick up some mice from the pet store soon."

****

"Hey, Joseph! How's it going, man? I haven't seen you around in a while."

The friendly greeting from the pet store clerk caught Dr. Carlson off guard. *I just want to buy the mice and get out of here. I don't need any friends.*

"Uh, yeah, well my old snake died and I didn't have one for a while so I didn't need any mice."

The store worker nodded. "We've got some really nice yellow rat snakes in the back if you're looking for a new one."

"No, no I already have one," the doctor replied. "I just need to get some mice for him."

"Where'd you get him? I probably know the person who sold him to you. Pet stores are a small industry, you know."

Irritation began to set in. *Stop being so curious and just give me the damn mice!*

"You wouldn't know it," Joseph said. "It was actually my sister's kid's snake. She lives in Blacksburg. Having the snake freaked out my little niece too much so they had to get rid of it."

More nodding from the bobble-headed employee. "Yeah, bro, that's a common story. Reptiles aren't for everybody - especially snakes." He turned and started to walk toward the aisle with the mice. "How many will you be getting today?"

"Three."

The clerk pulled the squirming little white rodents out of their cage and dropped them into a box. "Alright, there you go. That'll be $9. Still paying with cash?"

Joseph's shoulders tensed. "What?"

"I just remember from before that you always pay in cash. That's rare these days . . . everybody usually just wants to swipe their debit card and be done with it."

"Oh, well, I guess I'm old school. And yes, paying in cash."

FIVE

The clerk at the pet store had been bothering Joseph for several days. *He knows me by name. He knows I always pay in cash.* The next question wouldn't leave the doctor's mind: *does he know too much?*

Joseph's first idea was one that he had become increasingly comfortable with over the past two years. *I can just kill him.* If for some reason the FBI started to suspect Joseph, and God forbid showed his photo around the area or on television, the pet store clerk would immediately recognize him as 'the mice guy.' Not that Dr. Carlson couldn't easily explain away buying the mice. After all, he made no secret of the fact that he did medical research at his house. But questions would arise about why he lied regarding the purpose of the mice and why he always paid in cash. Then investigators would want to see the mice in his home lab. *Not an option*, he thought.

Yeah, Joseph nodded. *I'll just kill him.*

After work the next day, Joseph got in his car and, instead of driving home, made his way in the direction of the pet store. *This shouldn't take too long*, he thought. *Go in, shoot him, and leave.* The doctor nodded. *Simple.*

It took Joseph a few minutes to find a parking space, which was unusual in that particular shopping center. He didn't think much of it when he parked, tucked his gun in his jacket pocket, and walked to the store.

Much to Dr. Carlson's dismay, the pet shop was full of parents and children. *What the hell?*

Spotting his intended target behind the counter ringing up a sale, Joseph cut the line and walked up to the clerk. "What's going on here?"

The worker released a frustrated sigh. "Some genius with the local Boy Scouts decided his troop should earn an animal science patch by taking care of a fish for a month.

They all came here straight from their latest group meeting or whatever."

"How many of them are there?" asked Joseph. He wanted to know how long the unwelcome witnesses would be hanging around the store.

The clerk, mistaking Joseph's question for sympathy with his flood of fish-buying scouts, placed his hand on the doctor's shoulder. "I don't know bro. Too many of them if you ask me. I'm happy for the sales, but *dude*."

Dr. Carlson flinched under the other man's touch and instinctively stepped sideways. "Yeah . . . kids are annoying" was all he could manage to say.

Shit, Joseph thought. *This isn't going to work.* It wasn't simply the dozens of people around that put the brakes on his murder plans. Joseph had just noticed the security cameras in all four corners of the store. He sighed. *Better a possible potential tipster to deal with than a bunch of snot-nosed do-gooders and video evidence.*

"Look man," the clerk broke in, "I'm sorry it's so busy. I gotta ring these people up, so it could be ten or fifteen minutes before I can get to you."

Joseph shrugged as nonchalantly as he could. "You know what? Don't worry about it. The snake isn't going to starve if he doesn't eat today."

"You sure?"

"Yeah, no problem. Good luck with the brats," Carlson said. He then turned and weaved his way through the crowded store, more thankful than ever that he hadn't chosen to work in pediatrics. Much to Joseph's surprise, he wasn't all that upset about not getting to kill the store clerk. *I actually kind of like the guy*, he thought. *Dumbs as bricks, but I like him.*

Getting back into his car to drive home, Joseph laughed. "Good thing we didn't kill him."

SIX

The morning after Joseph decided not to kill the bumbling pet store worker, he was back at his office at the NIH. As with the last time he created a killer illness from scratch, Dr. Carlson was finding it increasingly difficult to keep up his good doctor Isaac personality at work when all he really wanted to do was be Joseph in his home lab. *It certainly helps that Isaac is already a fairly grumpy person. I never could understand why people want to be nice all the time.*

Speak of the devil, Joseph thought as Keri Dupree walked into his office.

"Hey Isaac, you still drive that Mercedes, right?" Keri asked.

Dr. Carlson was caught off guard by the question. "Umm, yeah. Why?"

"Scott is looking to get a new car. He wants a sports car but I'm trying to talk him into something a little more practical." She shook her head. "I mean you can't really fit a car seat in the front of a two-seater."

"Fair point."

"Do you like your car though? Would you recommend it? I'm trying to think ahead . . . before I know it Matty will be playing T-ball and all of that. Is it good for trunk space and traveling and all of that?"

It took all of Joseph's self-control to not burst out laughing. *Trunk room? Yeah, you can fit a body in there easily. Traveling? Sure - I've crisscrossed the country in my car.*

"Isaac?"

"Huh? Oh, yeah, great car. I don't have any complaints."

Keri seemed satisfied with her boss' answer. "You must like it if you've held on to it for so long. Heck, with the money you made on that last drug patent you could buy any car you wanted."

Dr. Carlson bristled at the mention of money. "Yes, I like my car. And I don't care about the money."

The subject of finances hit a raw nerve with Dr. Dupree. She and her lawyer husband certainly weren't hurting for money, but she knew that Isaac was sitting on millions of dollars. It bothered her. Even though she knew it was childish, Keri resented the fact that her boss made so much money but then said he didn't care about it. Feeling more combative than usual, Keri pressed: "usually a main reason why people work is to earn money so they can spend it."

Dr. Carlson didn't take the bait. "Like I said, I don't care about the money."

"You sell drug prototypes to big pharmaceutical companies for millions each but you don't care about the money?"

Joseph Isaac leaned back from his microscope to look over at Keri. "Just because you have a kid's college to save for now doesn't mean you can convince me you've gone mainstream. I research because I love it. I love the high that comes with it. With being the first person to discover something. And so do you, missy, so don't give me all that crap about money."

"Okay, okay, fine," Keri said, throwing her hands up in the air. "We won't talk about finances. We won't talk about how you've kept the same car for years and still live in a relatively modest house when you could afford a mansion."

Dr. Carlson was getting annoyed now, and it showed in his tone of voice. "It costs money to fund my research. I like my car, and it's only three years old. I also like my house. It's two stories with four bedrooms. I changed one of the bedrooms into a laboratory, but what do I need with all that extra space? Plus I like my neighborhood. It's quiet. People leave me alone."

Keri sighed. "Okay, you win. No more talking. We'll just work side-by-side sixty hours per week and only speak when absolutely necessary."

Carlson gave Keri a rare smile. "It only took you eleven years, but you finally figured it out."

Keri laughed. "You sound like such a grumpy old man. You do know you're only forty-six, right?"

Isaac glared at his assistant. She ignored him and kept talking. "That's the most I've ever heard you talk about your house, though. Eleven years and I've never been there."

"If you're fishing for an invitation, you're not going to get one."

"You've been to my house several times," Keri pressed.

"Yes, I have."

"Ugh, fine. Whatever. Remind me to nominate you to be the grumpy dwarf in the office production of *Snow White*."

SEVEN

An article in *People* magazine of all places gave Joseph the final factor he needed to create his bacteria. A full nine months after he first began work on the project, Dr. Carlson was still running into problems with antibiotics. There were so many different types and levels of drugs designed to kill bacteria that his little villain kept dying off too quickly. Joseph had created a couple of bacterial cultures that were fast-acting, lethal, and not traceable. But as soon as he exposed the diseases to antibiotics, they were destroyed. The last element on his wish list, untreatable, was proving to be very difficult. Until Joseph read the magazine article, that is.

Sitting in the waiting room of his dentist's office late one March afternoon, Dr. Carlson was bored and mindlessly started shuffling through a stack of magazines on the coffee table in front of him. The cover of the gossip rag caught his attention. It was a picture of some celebrity he didn't recognize, but the title said it all: 'New Hospital Danger from Superbugs.'

Quoting the CDC, the article read:

Antibiotic . . . drugs have been used so widely and for so long that the infectious organisms the antibiotics are designed to kill have adapted to them, making the drugs less effective. . . . Some microorganisms may develop resistance to a single antimicrobial agent (or related class of agent), while others develop resistance to several antimicrobial agents or classes. These organisms are often referred to as multidrug-resistant or MDR strains. In some cases, the microorganisms have become so resistant that no available antibiotics are effective against them.

Joseph read through the article and realized he had his answer. *'No available antibiotics are effective against them.' Of course. Why didn't I think of this before? It will make my disease more effective and at the same time confuse any investigators. They'll think it's just another superbug.* He nodded and smiled. *I've got it now.*

Throughout his teeth cleaning, Dr. Carlson's mind continued to run through his now-complete attack plan. *A specially designed, antibiotic resistant, flesh-eating bacteria. I'll dump it into the open-air water treatment plants in different cities and towns around the country, spreading out the victims. Yep,* the doctor thought. *This is going to work out just fine. Maybe even better than the last time.*

Blue-gray eyes sparkled beneath the glare of the dentist chair's light. The gleam in Joseph's eyes matched the wicked intent in his heart and the disturbing pictures in his head. People from across the country - dozens, hundreds, maybe even thousands - flooding into hospitals, all of them dying from the inside out as his own personal bacteria ate its way through their bodies.

The chatty dental hygienist flossing Dr. Carlson's teeth had no idea of the thoughts running through her patient's mind. *So many will die. And no one will ever know it was me.*

****

Several hours later, a cavity-free Joseph was back in his secret laboratory and ready to resume work on his bacteria. Dr. Carlson was renowned for his attention to detail, and he applied the same work ethic to the projects he didn't want anyone to know about. The medical researcher walked to the corner of the underground room and pressed his hand against the front of a small safe. After a quick fingerprint scan, the door popped open. Joseph tried to write down as little as possible during this project, but some things had to be put on paper.

"Like this," the doctor said, grabbing a small notepad from inside the safe. "All of the lessons I learned during Operation Respect."

Carlson flipped open the little book. "Lesson One," he said. "Local radio stations suck." Joseph groaned as he remembered the twenty-five miserable hours he spent driving to and from Denver, Colorado. Large sections of Middle America, where cows outnumbered people, were also home to nothing but country radio stations. After that trip, a satellite radio subscription became a necessary expense. *Lesson learned*, he thought.

"Number Two: role play ahead of time. Make sure you cover all of your bases." Several very tense moments during that same Colorado trip reinforced the importance of sweating the small stuff. When dropping off a box full of virus-tainted blood, Joseph had to fill out a donation form. *One contingency I hadn't planned on. I would've been seriously screwed if the receptionist checked the fake address I wrote down.* From then on, Dr. Carlson prepared a false identity - address included - for each blood drop.

"Lesson Three: know your enemy."

Joseph ran his hand through his close-cropped gray hair. "This is more important this time around. The attacks will be more concentrated. Even with the antibiotic-resistance thrown in, this is far less likely to be written off as some freak mutation."

Carlson turned his back to the safe and began pacing the floor of the small room. "I'm going to leave a trail. There's no way not to. Some pipsqueak FBI agent will put big pushpins on a map of all the places where people are getting sick. They'll figure out a pattern. A connection." He sighed, his eyes squinting in concentration. "I need a way to know more about what the police are going to do. Inside knowledge."

Joseph returned his small notebook to the safe and went about his usual evening work, this time with his focus on making the bacteria more resistant to antibiotics. Thoughts about the police investigation were never far from his mind, though. *I need a way to know. I need to sit down with a detective or an FBI agent or somebody like that and find out how they would investigate this.*

Carlson released a frustrated sigh. "I can't do that. As soon as the outbreaks actually started I would be the prime suspect." An uncharacteristic growl escaped Joseph's lips. And then, the next instant, he smiled. "Of course," he said aloud. "Why didn't I think of that before? Yeah," he nodded. "I know what I'll do."

EIGHT

James Leavey was the longest-serving instructor at the FBI's training Academy. Even though he was already sixty-two, the completely bald man still ran three miles every morning and took pride in the fact that his fitness test scores rivaled those of the fresh-faced recruits in his classes. Instructor Leavey's reputation around the Quantico, Virginia-based Academy was for being tough but fair, extremely knowledgeable, and one hundred percent dedicated to the Bureau. Other instructors were known to also use Leavey as a negative example from time to time - a picture of someone who was married to the job. James knew that the label fit; work-life balance had never been his strong suit. His one marriage was brief - eighteen months - and Sue had left when she realized she would always come in second to her husband's first love: the FBI.

So yes, technically speaking, Leavey was alone. But he never felt that way. Five days per week, fifty-one weeks per year, he was in a classroom full of young, bright minds eager to serve their country as federal agents. Leavey's fellow instructors were all sociable and courteous, and there was never a shortage of people to eat lunch with at the Academy's cafeteria. Indeed, when he went home at night, the forty-year Bureau veteran liked the peace and quiet of his empty house. His alone time gave him opportunities to read, watch old movies, and simply relax.

Yep, the instructor thought one morning as he walked back to his office from his first class, *life is good.*

A blinking red light on Leavey's desk phone told him he had a new voicemail. He put the phone on speaker, sat down in his chair, and loosened his tie.

"Hi," the message began, "this is Dr. Isaac Carlson from the National Institutes of Health in Bethesda. I got your number from the FBI Academy's website . . . I hope you don't mind. I'm calling to see if we could schedule a time to meet soon. I'm doing some research into police procedural tactics for a book and would love to pick your brain for a little while. My number is 301-555-8727. Thanks, and I hope to hear from you soon."

"Wow," Instructor Leavey said. "Isaac Carlson wants to talk to me?" James was of course familiar with Dr. Carlson - his work on the tainted blood outbreaks was taught as a case study in most counterterrorism classes at the Academy. "I wonder why he picked me?"

The wonder didn't last long, though. First a student knocked on Leavey's door with a question, followed by a colleague asking him to guest lecture the next week. *No rest for the weary,* Leavey thought an hour later when he rose to walk to his next class of the day.

****

It was a full ten hours later before James remembered the voicemail from that morning. Having stored Dr. Carlson's number into his cellphone, Leavey called him on his drive home.

"Isaac Carlson," a man answered.

"Hi, Dr. Carlson, this is James Leavey from the FBI Academy."

"Oh, yeah, hi," Joseph said, his voice softening once he knew who had called him. "Thanks for calling me back."

"No problem. So you said in your voicemail that you're writing a book?"

"Well, I'm thinking about it," the doctor said. "I wanted to get your opinion on a few things before I actually dive into it."

"Umm, yeah, okay." Leavey was still curious as to why a renowned medical researcher like Dr. Carlson would want his opinion on anything, but James wasn't going to turn him down without at least hearing him out.

On the other end of the line, Joseph breathed a sigh of relief. *It doesn't sound like he suspects anything.* "Great!" Joseph said. *Too much enthusiasm. Tone it down, Joe.* "I was thinking we could meet sometime this week after work to discuss it. Coffee or dinner or whatever."

Instructor Leavey started getting nervous. *This kinda sounds like a date.* Although it had been a while since he last had a girlfriend, James was most definitely straight. If not slightly homophobic.

Joseph's laughter broke Leavey's train of thought. "I just realized that it sounded like I was asking you out on a date. Sorry. Not my intention. A business meeting."

The FBI man exhaled. *Phew.* "Yeah, it was a little awkward there for a minute. But I would be happy to do a business meeting this week. How about Wednesday night? My last class ends every day at 6pm."

"Wednesday works for me," Joseph said. "You're doing me the favor so you can pick the location."

"Alright. There's a place called Smiling Tony's near the Academy. They make a mean lasagna. Let's say 6:30?"

"Perfect. I'm looking forward to it."

****

Traffic from the NIH headquarters in Bethesda, Maryland to the FBI Academy in Quantico, Virginia was notoriously brutal, and Joseph decided he should leave work by 4:45pm in order to not be late for his meeting with James Leavey. Dr. Carlson shrugged off Keri's good-natured ribbing about his leaving early and made the drive to Quantico in record time.

Joseph pulled his car into the parking lot of a one-story wooden building with a hand-painted sign on top that read 'Smilin' Tony's'. *This place has the best lasagna around?* He shook his head. *I doubt it.* The doctor then reached over into his passenger seat and grabbed the notepad and pen he would use to take notes during the meeting. "Need to make it look like this is legit," he said.

As he was climbing out of his car, Joseph saw a well-worn Jeep Cherokee pull into the lot. A man about twenty years Joseph's senior climbed out and hitched his khaki pants up higher on his waist. *That's my guy,* Dr. Carlson thought with a smile. *Hunter green SUV. Got it.* Joseph's smile turned to a laugh. *Sucker doesn't have any idea what he's walking into.* Joseph paused. *Remember, be nice. We want this guy to like us.*

Ten minutes later, the two men were seated at a corner booth and enjoying fresh-baked bread while waiting on their meals.

"So here's my basic idea," Dr. Carlson began. "I'm a doctor, as you know. I've wanted to write a novel for a while now, and I think I could do a pretty good job writing something like a medical thriller. The only problem is I don't know anything about police work. How to do an investigation, what the lingo is . . . all of that is foreign to me."

"Alright," Instructor Leavey replied. "So where do I come in?"

"I figure we might partner up on it. I can do the medical side and you can do the police side and then we joint publish them. Or, if you don't have time for that or don't like writing, I can just ask you questions about things in the story as they come up. What do you think?"

Leavey took another bite of bread and thought about it while chewing. "I'm not much of a writer, but I like the idea of a joint project. Could be fun. Maybe we work together on the ideas and the stories and then you do the writing? Splitting any royalties accordingly, obviously."

Joseph nodded. "Yeah, that works for me." He paused. "You sure your wife won't mind you taking on such a big project?"

"What wife?" Leavey laughed. "No man, I'm not married. No wife. No girlfriend. No kids. No pets."

"Look at that, another bachelor like me," Joseph replied with a grin. He lifted his glass for a toast. "To a life free from nagging women."

"Here here!"

The two men took a sip from their drinks and laughed again.

A waitress arrived carrying a tray with Leavey's lasagna and Joseph's chicken parmesan. After they started eating, the FBI man asked: "so why me? Surely there are other local police or even other FBI agents you could have asked to do the job."

Joseph nodded. "Yeah, probably. I did think about asking an FBI agent that I knew from the SuperAIDS case . . . I think her name was White. But I figured what I really need is somebody who knows police procedure like the back of his hand, and who better for that than an instructor at the FBI Academy? So I went to the website and saw that you're the longest-serving professor there."

"Well, that's not really saying much," Leavey answered. "I've only been teaching there for ten years. Everybody else just leaves the Academy for better paying jobs at big name universities."

Joseph was curious. "Why haven't you?"

Leavey shrugged his shoulders and took another bite of lasagna. "I like what I do. It's just me so it's not like I need more money to support a family or anything. Plus I've got a trick knee from some shrapnel I took in Vietnam, and the health benefits for federal employees are second to none." He grinned. "Although I don't have to tell you that, doctor."

The more the FBI instructor spoke, the more Joseph knew he had picked the right guy. *No wife to worry about him. No kids to call and check in. And if I take a hammer to that trick knee I bet he'll sing like a canary.* Joseph returned the other man's smile. "Yeah, the government does a pretty good job taking care of its own."

Knowing he needed to keep up the friendly facade, Dr. Carlson added: "so you served in Vietnam, huh?"

"Yep," Leavey nodded. "Two tours. That used to make me sound tough; saying I did two tours. Now we've got these kids over in Iraq and Afghanistan pulling three, four, five tours. It's ridiculous."

Joseph didn't really care about the service records of twenty-two year olds. He cared about himself, his mission, and getting as much information as possible out of Captain America here. Carlson shrugged. "Ridiculous, I guess. But it's not like they're drafted. They know what they're signing up for."

The FBI instructor acknowledged Dr. Carlson's comment with a bob of his head but offered no reply. It was rare to find a person nowadays who didn't give his or her full-fledged support to the troops, and the doctor's callous attitude toward the military members' sacrifices threw James off guard.

The doctor saw the look on Leavey's face and realized he had revealed a little too much of his true personality. *Time to wrap this up.* Quickly changing subjects, Joseph said: "okay, so I'll go home and start working on some story ideas. You know, the medical side of things. And then I'll give you a call sometime next week when I've put together a list of questions."

Instructor Leavey shrugged off his new acquaintance's remarks about the military and nodded his head in agreement. "Sounds good. I'll do some brainstorming of my own this weekend and see what I can come up with."

Dr. Carlson smiled. *Yes, you certainly will. Just not the kind of brainstorming you're thinking of now.*

NINE

Two days later, on Friday night, Joseph Carlson found himself back in Quantico, Virginia. He originally planned to kidnap James Leavey by sitting at the man's home and waiting for him to arrive from work, but Leavey's address was unlisted. Joseph knew it was risky to follow the FBI man all the way from the Academy to his house - the man was trained in investigation tactics, after all, and would probably notice if a car was tailing him. But Dr. Carlson didn't see any other option.

James Leavey didn't notice the silver sedan that followed him home from the Academy that Friday night. Having left work after his last class let out at six o'clock, the instructor's brain was on autopilot as he drove his green SUV to his modest house just north of Quantico. He pulled into his carport, climbed out of his car, and walked in the side door to his kitchen.

The instructor was just about to pour himself a beer when he heard a knock on the front door.

"Dr. Carlson. Umm, hi. I wasn't expecting you."

The visitor smiled. "I know, and I'm sorry to barge in like this. I just have a really great idea and got so excited about it that I wanted to tell you in person."

Instructor Leavey continued to block the front door. Something wasn't quite right about the situation . . . he just hadn't figured it out yet.

The doctor seemed to sense James' hesitation and took a step back on the front porch. "I'm sorry, I shouldn't have just shown up like this. I'll leave and we can just set up a different time to meet."

Leavey sighed. "No, you don't have to do that. Not after you took the time to drive all the way down here. Come on in." He stood back from the doorway and motioned for Dr. Carlson to enter the house. Leavey then started to walk back toward the kitchen. "I was just about to have a beer. You want one?"

"No thanks. I'm not much of a drinker."

Reaching his kitchen, James opened the refrigerator door and bent down to pick up a bottle of Bud Light. With his head still inside the fridge, Leavey paused. *Wait a minute. I never told him where I live.* The hairs on the back of the instructor's neck stood up straight and goose bumps covered his arms. Very slowly, he began to stand up.

"How did you - "

Leavey's question was cut short by the feeling of cool, hard metal being thrust into his ribs.

"Don't move," Dr. Carlson said. "Put the beer bottle down, back away from the refrigerator, and keep your hands where I can see them."

The older gentleman did as he was told. Although James had no doubt that he could defeat the scrawny Carlson in a fight, he was currently unarmed and wasn't dumb enough to do battle with a handgun stuck in his side.

"What do you want, Carlson?" he dared to ask.

"Shut up. I'll be the one asking the questions."

****

Despite his promise of questions, Joseph was silent as he escorted his hostage out of the man's house and to his car parked in the driveway. The doctor looked nervously around the neighborhood and, not seeing anyone, opened his trunk.

"Get in," Carlson said.

"You've gotta be kidding me," the instructor replied. He was beginning to regain some of his composure and confidence after the initial shock of the situation.

"Get. In," Joseph repeated, digging his gun deeper into the other man's side.

Leavey winced and then complied, crawling into the trunk of Dr. Carlson's sedan and praying that one of his neighbors would see what was happening. The FBI man knew that was a long shot, though, since his house was in a quiet cul-de-sac and the only people who wouldn't still be at work were a couple in their nineties who couldn't see three feet in front of them, let alone all the way across the street.

Once his hostage was curled up in the back end of his car, Joseph doused a dish rag with the chloroform he had brought with him. He then covered Leavey's nose and mouth with it, ensuring that the man wouldn't cause any problems during the drive from Quantico to North Bethesda.

When they arrived at Joseph's house, he was careful to pull all the way into his garage and close the door behind him before telling Leavey to get out of the car. Joseph didn't want any of his neighbors to see that he had company. The two men entered Carlson's home and walked directly to his kitchen, where Joseph punched a code into the keypad hidden under the edge of his granite countertop. The doctor saw the look of surprise on Leavey's face when the island's cabinet made a popping sound and then opened slightly on the end to reveal the stairs into the basement lab. *Welcome to my dungeon*, Joseph thought with glee. He then forced his hostage into the basement, careful to close and lock the door behind them. *We can't be having any Peyton Finch repeats.*

Dr. Carlson knew it was a risk to divulge his entire plan to the FBI instructor that he was tying to a chair in the middle of the underground bunker, but he didn't feel like he had any other choice. If Leavey didn't know the whole scheme, he wouldn't be able to give a full answer as to how the FBI would investigate it. So Joseph told the man everything: about the flesh eating bacteria, about its antibiotic resistant composition, and about the plan to dump the illness into water treatment plants so that it could spread throughout cities and towns.

The entire time Joseph was talking, James Leavey just stared at him, his eyes hardened and his jaw set. *Getting him to talk might be a bit more difficult than I thought,* Joseph worried.

TEN

Instructor Leavey wasn't exactly sure how to handle this situation. None of the normal rules applied. Usually, as a hostage, he would try to develop a rapport with his kidnapper so that hopefully, in the event of an escape or rescue attempt, the bad guy might think twice about shooting him. That split second hesitation could be the difference between life and death.

But there would be no rescue attempts, because no one knew he was there. Wherever 'there' was. A lifetime of putting the job above all else meant that there was no one waiting at home for him. No wife. No kids who might call to check in. All of his friends were also instructors at the FBI Academy, and he wasn't expected back at work until Monday morning. *Over forty-eight hours from now.*

Leavey also knew there was also little point in establishing a rapport or trying to talk Dr. Carlson down from his craziness. When lecturing on how to profile serial killers, Leavey always told his students that there was a fine line between genius and insanity. *And this guy has definitely crossed it*, he thought. *He can't let me live. I know all of his plans now.* "I'm on borrowed time," he whispered under his breath.

"What's that?" Joseph asked.

"Nothing. I just said I wonder what the time is," Leavey lied.

"It's time for you to talk, that's what time it is. I need to know how the FBI agents think. How you teach them to think. I don't want to be one step ahead; I want to be five steps ahead.

"Now this can be very easy or very hard. It's completely up to you," Joseph continued, cracking his knuckles as he walked toward the chair where his kidnapping victim was tied. "You tell me how the FBI conducts its investigations, and I'll be nice. You don't tell me, and things will get very painful very quickly."

Unlike his previous four kidnappings, the man seated in front of Joseph right then showed no fear. In fact, the seasoned FBI instructor wasn't displaying any emotion at all.

"Taking the hard road, huh?" Joseph said, trying his best to imitate the villains he saw on TV and in movies. Killing people was easy - Joseph knew how to do that. But beating them up? Torturing them? Joseph's only experience with physical violence of that sort was when he had been on the receiving end of it at school.

Channeling his inner tough guy, Joseph pulled his right arm back, made a fist, and punched James Leavey square in the nose.

A high-pitched, muffled cry of pain filled the room, but it wasn't coming from the man who now had a bloody nose. Joseph continued to scream through gritted teeth as he shook his hand, trying desperately to relieve the pain.

His hostage laughed. "First time you punched somebody? Hurts like the dickens, right?"

The other man's laughter infuriated Dr. Carlson. "Shut the hell up!" he yelled, grabbing a metal storage canister with his good hand and slamming it into the side of Leavey's face. This time it was the FBI man's turn to grimace in pain. "Who's laughing now, huh?" asked Joseph with a grin.

Dr. Carlson then took a minute to collect himself. He breathed deeply and straightened out his starched white Oxford shirt, all the while flexing his still-throbbing right hand.

"Let's try this again," the doctor proposed. "I say 'how does the FBI conduct its investigations,' and you say the answer. Ready? How does the FBI conduct its investigations?"

"The answer."

Once again Joseph grabbed the empty metal can and swung it straight into the side of his victim's head. "Not funny, you piece of shit. Now tell me the answer!"

"You know we talk about you at the FBI Academy, right?"

The question caught Joseph off guard. "What?"

"We talk about you. About biological attacks and how your team did such a great job with the whole SuperAIDS thing." He paused. "Then again, now that I think about it, it must've been pretty easy to solve a mystery that you created."

If Leavey had looked closely enough, the steam was almost literally visible as it came out of Joseph's ears. "If I want your opinion, I'll ask for it," he growled. "Now answer the damn question."

"I'm sorry, what was it again? I forgot."

This time, as punishment, Joseph walked to his desk, picked up a box of heavy research supplies, and brought it back to the middle of the room. He then dropped the box straight down on Instructor Leavey's foot. "Do you remember now?"

The older of the two men scrunched up his face in pain but didn't scream. When the shooting agony in his foot subsided, he sighed. "Look, can I ask you something?"

"No!"

"C'mon, that's a simple request. There's no reason for you to not agree to it. You're creating more conflict - making it even less likely that your hostage will give you the information you want."

Joseph realized that the instructor was correct. "Okay, fine. What's your question?"

"Why did you go through all of the trouble to kidnap me if all you wanted to know was FBI investigation tactics? There are hundreds, if not thousands, of books and websites out there that talk about it. Or, for that matter, you could've just kept up the book charade you started with and I probably would've told you everything you wanted to know."

"Not good enough. I want it applied to a certain scenario."

Leavey nodded his head in understanding. "Right. Of course. You want me to tell you how the Bureau will react to your cockamamie water poisoning scheme."

"It's not cockamamie," Joseph said. "And yes, that's what I want."

"And after I talk you're going to kill me."

"Right again," Joseph answered.

"Wrong again," Leavey replied. "Now I have zero reason to cooperate. Not to mention a heavy incentive to give you false information."

Joseph smiled. "I thought you might say that." Walking over to the small refrigerator in the corner, the same one that previously held bags of infected blood, Joseph opened the door and picked out a large syringe full of a clear liquid. "Do you know what amobarbital is, Instructor Leavey?"

"Truth serum."

"That's right," Dr. Carlson grinned, tapping the side of the syringe with his finger. "Truth serum. You're going to tell me what I need to know . . . whether you want to or not."

ELEVEN

Joseph injected the kidnapped FBI instructor with enough truth serum for a man twice his size, waited for it to enter the bloodstream, and then began peppering James Leavey with questions.

"What's the first thing you do in an investigation?"

"What kinds of clues will the FBI be looking for?"

"What is the biggest mistake that people make when committing crimes?"

Joseph was careful to say 'people who commit crimes' instead of 'criminals.' It was a small difference, only semantics, but it mattered to him. *I'm not a criminal. Criminals are thugs who steal cars or beat up old ladies. I'm a well-respected doctor with a purpose behind my actions. Call me a terrorist . . . fine. But I'm not a criminal.*

Unfortunately for Joseph, the effects of the truth serum wore off after a couple of hours and Leavey fell asleep well before his captor was satisfied with the man's answers. Exhausted after a long day of work, kidnapping, and questioning, Dr. Carlson checked the restraints on his sleeping hostage's chair and then trudged up out of the basement to get some sleep himself. Joseph was careful to lock the secret door behind him, ensuring that his houseguest wouldn't be going anywhere without permission.

****

After getting a few restless hours of sleep, Joseph was back down in his secret lab-turned-holding cell trying to get more information out of his smart-mouthed FBI instructor.

"Should've bought more truth serum," the unbreakable Leavey sneered.

"I have other ways of extracting information," replied Joseph.

"Oh yeah? What, are you going to try to punch me again? Because that worked so well the first time."

A very frustrated Dr. Carlson winced at the reminder of his bruised and swollen right hand. "Why aren't you cooperating? Everybody else I've kidnapped has been afraid of me."

The agent was surprised to learn that the esteemed Dr. Isaac Carlson had done something like this before.

"Fear implies options," Leavey finally answered. "Those people must have thought there was a chance you wouldn't kill them, and they were afraid of option number two wherein they died. You already told me you're going to kill me. I have no reason to doubt that. Since my only option is death, it's kind of stupid for me to be afraid of it."

Joseph squinted his eyes together behind his glasses and tried to process the other man's reasoning. "You're very weird," he finally concluded.

"You're one to talk."

Dr. Carlson let loose a loud, frustrated scream.

"Enough!" he yelled. "I'm tired, I'm annoyed, and I just want to get this over with. Before the drugs wore off you said that they would map all of the bacterial outbreak locations to try to find a pattern. Then what?"

"Then you can kiss my ass."

"That's it," Joseph said. Picking up a plastic razor from the worktable beside him, Carlson walked up and stood inches away from James Leavey, pressing the thin, silver blade of the razor into the side of the other man's face.

"Then what?" he repeated.

When Leavey didn't respond, Joseph dug the razor even deeper into his skin and jerked it down, slicing open his hostage's face from cheekbone to chin.

The FBI instructor's wails of pain filled the room, but still he gave Joseph no answer.

"How about the other side then?" asked the doctor. "Even you out so the two match."

Looking at the nearly three-inch gashes on either side of the instructor's face was hard for even Joseph to stomach, but he knew he couldn't stop now. Plus, a part of him kind of liked it. He liked the power.

"You see, Leavey, you were wrong. You did have options. You could've told me what I wanted to know and died quickly and painlessly. But no, you chose to not cooperate. So I have to use alternative methods of persuasion." Joseph smiled. "What was it that the military called it? Enhanced interrogation?" He laughed. "I bet you might've even taught your students some of that."

A light bulb then went off in the doctor's head. "You clearly have a high tolerance for pain. Let's see how you handle drowning."

****

James Leavey watched, horrified, as his kidnapper walked over to a sink and filled a large bucket with water. The doctor then picked up a dish towel and his gun and walked to stand in front of the FBI instructor.

Joseph temporarily put his 9mm Beretta on the ground, only long enough to re-tie the agent's hands and feet to make sure he couldn't pull free. The doctor then walked around behind the plastic folding chair and leaned it back so that Agent Leavey's head was on the ground and his feet were sticking up in the air.

Leavey felt the blood begin rushing to the top half of his body but he didn't care. *I'm as good as dead now anyway. Even if I did by superhuman miracle manage to get free and overpower him, the door out of here is sealed and the room is soundproofed. There's no point in trying.*

Allowing himself the brief luxury of surrender, James noticed how good the cool concrete felt against the back of his head. He closed his eyes and was more relaxed than he had been since this whole ordeal started.

"Don't try any funny stuff," his tormentor's voice rang out. "I've got my gun pointed at you the whole time."

Leavey heard the words but wasn't really listening. After sitting upright for what seemed like forever, it felt amazing to (sort of) lie down. James was quickly on his way to falling asleep. *That would be good,* he thought. *Just fall asleep and not wake up.*

The FBI man then felt a towel being placed over his face. Searing pain returned when the coarse fabric fibers landed on his freshly-cut cheeks. Before he had a chance to scream, though, Leavey began to choke as an endless amount of water was poured over his face.

He shook his head frantically, trying in vain to both keep his mouth closed and breathe for air at the same time. Wave upon wave of water rained down on James' face. He felt it go up his nose then down his windpipe into his lungs. The instructor's chest started to hurt as the air remaining in his lungs wanted to escape but his desperate body fought to keep it in.

More water brought on more choking and more pain, both in his lungs and in the raw razor blade gashes on his face. James tried to think of something beyond air; tried to remind himself that Dr. Carlson still needed him alive.

He won't actually kill me yet. He won't actually kill me yet. Leavey opened his mouth to cough out water but only succeeded in allowing more in. *What the hell am I saying? He doesn't know what he's doing. He's going to kill me now by accident!*

Suddenly, the water stopped. Leavey's lungs were on fire and he started gasping for air, almost wheezing as he sucked in more and more precious oxygen. In the background, he heard water running and knew that the reprieve wouldn't last long.

He was right. The evil doctor's bucket was refilled and the torture resumed.

The instructor's body went into panic. He tried to vomit out water from his stomach, but the liquid simply hit the towel over James' face and went right back down into his mouth, causing the FBI man to choke even more. Fear came to him just as quickly as the water, rushing through his mind and body. *Okay, God, I know we don't talk much but please for the love of, well, you . . . make it stop!*

As if on cue, the water ceased and the wet towel was removed.

The sound of wheezing and coughing filled the small underground room. Another noise was also present: Joseph's laughter.

The FBI instructor's initial feeling of relief was overtaken by anger.

"You stupid piece of shit!" he yelled. "I almost drowned, you bastard!" The screaming was made less effective by his frequent stops to cough and gasp for more air. "What good would that do you if I drowned, huh? Then you definitely wouldn't get your answers, you sick fuck!"

Two evil eyes glared back down at James. "How's your stomach?" the doctor asked. "Pretty full of water right now? So I guess it wouldn't feel too good if I took my foot and did this," he said, stepping down hard on Leavey's midsection.

Water flew up from the torture victim's stomach and out of his mouth, only to be caught by gravity and land back on his soaked, bleeding face.

The glare turned to a grin. "I think I'll just let that fester for a few minutes while I go eat some breakfast."

Dr. Carlson then turned and walked up the stairs leading out of the secret room, leaving his latest victim alone on the floor - tired, wet, bleeding, and furious.

TWELVE

Thirty minutes later, Joseph returned to his torture chamber to find Instructor Leavey asleep. Walking over to where the man's chair was still lying back on the ground, Dr. Carlson leaned down and yelled in his ear: "wake up!"

Leavey's eyes shot open and he resumed coughing as his body tried to rid itself of the remaining water. Joseph also noticed the yellow stains on the front of his captive's pants. *Hours on end with no bathroom break, that's what happens,* Joseph concluded.

The doctor knew he needed his kidnapping victim sitting up for their next chat, but it was a struggle for the slightly-built doctor to lift the FBI man's chair up from the floor into its proper seated position.

The instructor's short nap had recharged both his batteries and his mouth. "Need to hit the weights a little more, Carlson."

"Shut up, vomit face. I've had about enough of you and your smart mouth."

Leavey cringed. He knew the moniker was true. The blood that had at one point been streaming out of the gashes on his face was washed away during the waterboarding, and all that remained now was raw, red hamburger flesh and dried vomit. Thankfully, James had managed to catch his breath and stop heaving after the two prolonged rounds of simulated drowning. His lungs still burned, though, going off like firecrackers anytime some of the lingering water in them tried to cough its way out.

The tired, bloodied, and bruised FBI man began waging an internal battle with himself. The little angel on his right shoulder congratulated him. *You've done so well! You haven't given him any information, except when he drugged you. You haven't been broken yet. Stay strong!* The devil on his left shoulder, though, complete with a red cape and horns, wanted nothing more than for Instructor Leavey to give in. *Enough already! Just tell him what he wants to hear so he'll stop. He's going to kill you, he's going to kill other people, so just make it as painless for you as possible.*

The debating shoulder minions stopped when they saw Joseph's next torture device. The doctor had once again walked behind James to the other side of the room, only to return a few minutes later with a box of matches and a small pack of sewing needles.

Leavey's eyes followed his captor's every move, staring as the man lit a match and ran a needle up and down the flame in what looked like a sterilization technique.

The madman's eyes met his victim's - evil crossing with pain, happiness with fear. *The sick bastard is actually enjoying this.* That realization hit the instructor hard. *It takes a special kind of psycho to genuinely enjoy torturing people.*

Joseph slowly walked over to the chair where the federal agent was still tied. Grabbing the man's left index finger, Carlson took the sharp end of the two-inch needle and jammed it up and under Leavey's nail, as far as he could make it go.

The scream that James Leavey unleashed was unlike anything Joseph had ever heard before. Bone chilling, blood curdling, hair raising cries of pure agony. Tears flowed steadily out of the man's eyes, the salt falling into his open facial wounds and causing the screams to increase their horrifying volume.

"Was one not enough?" Joseph asked above the noise, lighting another match to sterilize a second needle, a force of habit embedded by decades of medical practice.

Dr. Carlson blew out the second match and tossed it on the ground. He then took hold of James' right index finger and injected half the length of the needle into the mushy skin just below the man's nail.

The only reason that the screams didn't return was because they had never stopped.

The sixty-two year old FBI agent suddenly ceased to make any sounds, his eyelids fluttering rapidly just before his eyes and head rolled backwards.

"Nice one, Joseph," the doctor scolded himself. "You induced a vasovagal syncope . . . he passed out from the pain."

Dr. Carlson shook his head in frustration, yanked the two needles out of his hostage's fingers, and began cleaning up some of the mess that the morning's events had created in his lab. "Fuck it," he said. "This is too much hassle. I'll use what he told me and the rest I'll just figure out on my own."

Walking back over to his workstation, Joseph opened a drawer and pulled out a syringe full of the same tranquilizer he had used to knock out eight-year-old Peyton Finch several years earlier.

"Time for a little nap," the doctor cooed. "Then tonight, I'll take you out to this great spot I know in a national park. Very secluded. Quiet. Great place to dig a grave."

Joseph stabbed his victim in the shoulder with the needle, gave the arm a pat, and walked back up the stairs and out of his basement lab.

"There's a special place in Hell for people like him," the angel on James Leavey's shoulder whispered.

"I agree," the demon answered back.

THIRTEEN

Well over two years had passed between Joseph's last visit to Blue Mountain National Park and this one. And while some of the circumstances were changed, his core mission was the same: dispose of a body.

It still amazed Dr. Carlson that the three homeless people's bodies hadn't been found. Even after little Peyton Finch was unearthed, the FBI and U.S. Park Police still managed to miss the three other graves right in the same area. *Not the sharpest knives in the drawer*, Joseph thought. He then unloaded the tools he would need from his trunk. Shovel: check. Gun: check. Flashlight: check. *At least this time I don't have to drain the blood from his body. Wouldn't do me much good, anyway, since I injected all of the truth serum into him.*

Closing the trunk, Joseph picked up the shovel in one gloved hand and his pistol in the other. He then walked around to the passenger side of his car. Opening the door, Dr. Carlson pointed the gun at Instructor Leavey's head. "Get out."

The tormented FBI teacher had little choice but to comply. Enough brain power remained for him to rub off as much of his blood onto the seat as he could and place his handcuffed fingers firmly on the dashboard and door handle as he pulled himself up and out of the car. *At least they'll know I was here*, he thought.

Joseph handed the shovel to his hostage. But, when Leavey tried to grip and hold it, the heavy tool fell out of his grasp and clanged loudly against the parking lot pavement.

The rational side of Dr. Carlson knew that the other man simply didn't have enough energy left to hold the shovel, but the other side of him didn't care.

"What the hell are you doing? You think if you drop it loudly enough somebody will hear you? Newsflash:

nobody's out here. Nobody can hear you. Nobody can save you."

Joseph stuck his gun into Leavey's ribcage. "Now start walking."

****

Park Ranger Peter Kine was surprised to see a car in the parking lot of one of the least-visited areas of Blue Mountain National Park. He was even more surprised to see it there at three o'clock in the morning.

"Uhh, Joan?" he called in on his radio. It was a few minutes before his fellow night shift staffer responded.

"Yeah Pete, what is it?"

"You know people who work graveyard for Baltimore PD, right?"

"Yeah . . ."

"I need you to call over there," said Ranger Kine. "There's an empty car out here in Lot F. It's a pretty nice model too. I want to make sure it hasn't been stolen."

Peter's counterpart was excited by the prospect of something interesting happening during her usually boring shift. "Absolutely, yeah. I'll call over there now. What's the plate number?"

****

Joseph was in a great mood as he walked through the trails leading out of the woods after he buried Agent Leavey. He now knew significantly more about how the FBI would try to track him, which would help tremendously in the coming months. Plus, it felt really good to kill the smartass instructor. Joseph had missed that feeling. The rush that came with fresh death. Like an addict, the doctor had just scored a big hit and was still riding the high while he trekked towards the parking lot.

Car headlights stopped him. The high immediately ended. *It's 3am. Nobody in their right mind would be out here right now*, Joseph thought. *Except the cops. And look at me: walking out of the woods, alone, carrying a shovel and a gun.*

Dr. Carlson threw his shovel into the heavy brush alongside the trail. His first instinct was to chuck the gun as well, but he knew better than that. It was registered to him. Instead, he double-checked to make sure the safety was on and then shoved the pistol down into his boot.

Confident that he no longer looked like a serial killer, Joseph resumed the walk to his car.

****

The sound of footsteps crunching over dirt and sticks made the park ranger jump. His hand instinctively moved to his gun holster, ready for whoever or whatever might be coming out of the woods. With his free hand, Ranger Kine shone his flashlight toward the direction of the noise. "Who's there?"

The ranger was relieved when a skinny, middle-aged white guy in khakis and a golf shirt came walking out of the woods. "Don't shoot!" were the man's first words.

Kine was a little less on edge due to the man's size and appearance, but he remained skeptical. "Are you Joseph Isaac Carlson, Jr.?" he asked, repeating the name of the vehicle's owner that Joan had given him.

Joseph froze. *How the hell does he know that?* Carlson was happy that it was dark enough and he was still far away enough that the uniformed official couldn't see the panic on his face. The words of James Leavey came rushing back into Joseph's mind. "We're very good at spotting liars. People get in trouble when they lie about stupid stuff; stuff they don't need to lie about."

So Joseph decided to tell the truth. For now.

"Yes," he replied. "I'm Dr. Carlson. Although people call me Isaac."

The other man had come close enough now that Joseph could see he was a park ranger. *Hopefully because he was too stupid to get into the police academy.*

Ranger Kine lowered his flashlight. "So that's your car?" he asked, gesturing over his shoulder to Joseph's sedan.

"Yep."

"It's three o'clock in the morning, Dr. Carlson. What are you doing out in the woods at this hour?"

Joseph decided to play the Aww-Shucks-I'm-A-Doctor card. He shrugged his shoulders. "I know it's probably not the best of ideas, but I'm working on a really big case right now and I've hit a mental block. I like to come out here on the weekends sometimes, so I figured a hike right now might clear my head."

"In the middle of the night?"

Joseph grinned sheepishly. "Like I said, maybe not the best of ideas."

The park ranger squinted his eyes and stared at Joseph, trying to decide if he was going to believe him or not. After what to Carlson seemed like an eternity, the man relaxed.

"Okay, doctor. You're right, not a smart thing to do. All kinds of wild animals live out here, you could get lost in the dark . . . and not to scare you away, but we did have a dead body recovered here a couple years ago. A little girl who was murdered and then buried out in the woods."

Joseph forced a look of surprise onto his face. "Oh wow. That's terrible."

Ranger Kine nodded. "It was. I'm going to let you go, Dr. Carlson. But consider this your verbal warning. Park hours are dawn to dusk. No exceptions."

"Understood. And thank you. I'll head home now."

"Good," Peter Kine replied.

He watched as the doctor got back into his car and drove away.

"All taken care of, Joan," the ranger said into his radio receiver. "The owner of the car came back. He had been hiking in the woods."

"At this hour?" she asked. "Is he crazy?"

"Probably."

FOURTEEN

Interrogation over and body safely buried, Dr. Carlson returned home to make a list of everything he learned from Detective Leavey.

"First," Joseph said, sitting down on his couch with a pen and paper, "is the suspect list. They'll see who had motive and opportunity. So I have to make sure I fit in neither category."

The doctor scribbled 'avoid M&O list' on the paper, followed by things he should do to accomplish that goal. "To begin with, tell no one our plans. Check. Next, make sure there's no way to trace us being at those drop locations. What was it that Leavey said? Google Maps searches and cell phone tower pings?" He remembered the FBI instructor's words: "Google is watching. Google knows."

I use an old-fashioned Atlas so we're safe there. Joseph relaxed a little bit. *And I'll leave my cell phone at home so they can't trace it.* "Perfect."

The doctor made a small mark next to each category. "Leavey also said they look into people's finances, but I'm not getting paid to do this, so all clear. Check," he said again. "And just like last time, I've been withdrawing cash in small amounts so I'll have enough for the trips. Check check."

Joseph stood up from the couch and walked over to the cabinet where he stored his Atlas. "Now for the tricky part. Leavey said they'll chart the outbreak spots to see if they can pinpoint a central location where the attacker is traveling from. Which means," Carlson said, flipping open the book to a map of the United States, "we need to make that central location look like someplace other than here."

****

Joseph settled on a small town in Pennsylvania called Halliston. Around three hours north of Bethesda, the former mining village would allow Dr. Carlson to do a test run with his bacteria before embarking on any longer, multiple-city trips. He also discovered, after some research, that Halliston's water treatment facility was located at the end of an otherwise vacant dirt road and secured only by a single padlocked chain. *Perfect.*

A year after he first started working on the flesh-eating illness, two years after the SuperAIDS outbreak, and four years after he first made the part-time switch from Isaac back to Joseph, Dr. Carlson's second killer disease was ready to go. On a warm Friday evening in early June, Joseph loaded a cooler full of bacteria vials into the trunk of his car and set off in the direction of Halliston.

FIFTEEN

A fourth-generation resident of Halliston, Pennsylvania, Bill Davis liked to think of himself as a throwback to a bygone era of football coaches: tough, demanding, perfectionist. Coach Davis expected more of his high school players, and expected his players to expect more of themselves.

There had been many a player and parent over the years who bristled at his tactics. Long practices, harsh - often foul - language, and an unrelenting focus on discipline. But when players who didn't like him left the team, there was never a shortage of boys waiting to fill the spots. Because there was something else that the Halliston High School football team was known for: winning.

And so it was that fifty-three year old Bill Davis and his coaching staff found themselves running conditioning drills one sweltering June morning. The workouts were supposedly optional, but, then again, so was making the team.

"Damn," said Chris Gryszkowich, the running backs coach. All of the other men nodded their heads in agreement with Coach Grizz's one-word description of the weather. At half-past eight in the morning, it was already nearing eighty degrees.

"Lots of water breaks today, gentlemen," ordered Coach Davis. He may have been tough, but he wasn't stupid. Bill genuinely wanted what was best for his players, and that didn't include a heat stroke. "Use the hoses," he clarified. There would be water, and an athletic trainer watching the workouts, but the boys would also drink straight from a hose. Old school. Just like their head coach.

An hour and fifteen minutes and two water breaks later, the first Halliston Tiger stopped mid-drill, took off his helmet, and threw up on the field.

"Jones!" Coach Davis yelled. "What the hell are you doing? Don't puke on my fresh cut grass!" He added: "go see the trainer. Get some water."

The coaches moved their agility drills to the other end of the football field and gave the student manager the unfortunate task of cleaning up the vomit. But before the team could resume their activities, another player lost his breakfast. Then another. A fourth boy ran off the field in the direction of the locker room, claiming something about needing a bathroom.

What the hell is going on? Coach Davis wondered.

****

"What in the world is this?"

The question asked by the surgical intern at Central Hospital in Halliston, Pennsylvania was the same one echoing through the minds of every other person in the emergency room. Including the Chief of Surgical Staff, a short, square man with short, square hair who had seen some wicked things during his years as a member of Doctors Without Borders. Dr. Rowe had grown accustomed to the fairly standard fare of influenzas and car wrecks in his sleepy bedroom community, but the wave of teenage boys flooding his hospital right then rivaled anything he had seen overseas.

It seemed like the entire Tigers football team had descended upon Central at once, and all of them with the same symptoms.

Red, feverish faces contrasted with pale, clammy hands and feet. The front of the boys' practice jerseys bore the yellowish-brown hallmarks of repeated vomiting, not to be outdone by the browned backsides of their practice pants.

"It's coming out both ends" was how the ambulance medic carrying the first patient had described it, and, while vulgar, it was accurate.

The hospital staff sprang into action, even though they were quickly overwhelmed and began sending other non-critical, unrelated patients to the next closest hospital a few towns over.

"I want everyone in here wearing gloves and masks!" Chief Rowe ordered. "I don't need my staff getting sick with this too . . . whatever this is."

He then grabbed the arm of his chief resident to get her attention. "Listen, I want them all on NS or LR to prevent dehydration, but at the same time hook them up to Zofran to try and stop the nausea. Run the anti-nausea at a faster rate than the other."

The younger doctor nodded. "Understood. We're on it."

****

An hour later, the hospital staff had exhausted all of their usual testing procedures. Complete blood counts were run and urine samples obtained from the few players who weren't already too dehydrated. "And still," Dr. Rowe shook his head, "we've got nothing."

Fifteen members of the Halliston High School football team and coaching staff were now patients in his hospital, all of them had the same symptoms, and no one knew why.

Dr. Rowe donned a mask and gloves and entered the room of one of the most critical patients, a strapping young athlete named Tyler Jones. Tyler's mom and dad were both beside their son's hospital bed and looked up when the doctor walked in.

"Any news?" the mother asked.

"I'm sorry, no. We're still running tests," the surgeon replied. "If you wouldn't mind leaving the room for a minute, I'd like to examine your son."

Mr. and Mrs. Jones didn't move.

"Please, I know you don't want to leave him, but you can stand right outside the door. It will only take a few minutes."

When the parents finally left the room, Dr. Rowe walked closer to the sick teenager to get a better look at his patient.

The boy's skin was red and swollen and, as his doctor quickly learned, hot to the touch. He also had goose bumps, the consequence of the fever and chills that were battling for control of Tyler's body.

Dr. Rowe listed off all of the patient's symptoms. "Vomiting. Diarrhea. Fever. Chills. Hot, swollen skin." He sighed. "What the hell is this?"

On a hunch, the doctor walked to the end of the hospital bed and lifted up the blanket covering Tyler's feet.

"Shit." Dr. Rowe instinctively took a step back from the bed and away from the scene in front of him. The young football player's toes were all in various stages of turning black, and his toenails had begun a yellowing process.

"How the hell did he get gangrene? He was perfectly healthy five hours ago."

A thought came to Dr. Rowe. He had only seen the disease once before in one patient in Africa. The doctor placed the bed linens back over Tyler's feet and then asked the boy's parents to come into the room.

"I want to go check on the other patients," Rowe said, "but first I just have one quick question. Has your son gone swimming any recently?"

"Just at the neighborhood pool," replied Mrs. Jones. "Why?"

"I was just wondering. I'll be back around to check on Tyler as soon as I can. If you need anything, there's always a nurse right outside."

Exiting the room, Dr. Rowe walked over to the nurses' station. "Get the surgical interns up here. I need them to start running full body CT scans on all of the football players and coaches. Also check all of them for gangrene, and do skin cultures on any visible infection sites." The doctor lowered his voice. "I think we might be dealing with a flesh-eating bacteria."

SIXTEEN

After giving instructions to his doctors and nurses, Chief Rowe went to his office and pulled up the internet on his computer. Necrotizing fasciitis, commonly known as flesh-eating bacteria, was a rare affliction and the doctor wanted to double check his symptoms and testing procedures.

Reading through the Centers for Disease Control's website, Dr. Rowe's suspicions grew.

"Fast acting?" he said aloud. "Yep."

"Fever? Check."

"Red, swollen skin with blisters or black spots? Yep, got that too."

The doctor sighed. "Throw in the vomiting, the diarrhea, and the severe pain, and we've got necrotizing fasciitis."

Frustrated, Dr. Rowe stood up from his desk and walked to the office window that overlooked the hospital's atrium. *It doesn't make any sense*, he thought. *The CBCs would have come back positive for one of the bacteria that can cause NF. And why have so many people gotten it all at once?*

A knock on the door broke his thoughts. "Excuse me, Chief?" an attending surgeon said.

"Yes?"

"We have the results back from the CT scans. You're going to want to come see this."

****

While Dr. Rowe and his staff examined the test results, Coach Davis made his way down the hallway of the local hospital, past the waiting room full of classmates, family, and friends of his players. They were all wondering the same thing he was: *what happened?*

One minute he and his coaches were conducting drills, and the next players were dropping like flies. Vomiting all over his field and writhing on the ground in pain.

Three hours later, after answering questions from his athletic director, school principal, and several very angry school board members, Coach Davis had finally managed to arrive at the hospital.

The overwhelmed doctors and nurses weren't allowing any non-family visitors, but Bill Davis was an exception. Football was king in Halliston, which meant that Halliston High's head coach sat on the throne. *Heavy is the head which wears the crown*, Bill thought, knocking softly before opening the door in front of him.

Coach Davis' first stop was to the room of the first player who fell ill, star linebacker Tyler Jones.

"T-Pain, how are you big guy?" he asked, using the nickname that Tyler's teammates had given him. It was appropriate since the Jones boy was known for leveling the boom against his opponents.

"Sick," the high schooler answered, his energy and spirits drained after everything his body had been through in the past several hours.

"I'm so sorry, Tyler. I have no idea what happened."

"Neither do the doctors," Tyler's dad interrupted. Chuck Jones was a foreman for a local construction company and not known for mincing his words. "My boy is here puking his guts out, with pain shooting through his arms and legs, and the doctors don't know a damn thing. They're running tests," he said, putting the word 'tests' in air quotes. "All they'll tell us is that they're running tests."

SEVENTEEN

Church services in Halliston the next morning were full of prayers for the health and healing of the football team. Priests and pastors were careful to add 'Thy will be done' at the end of the line, but no one wanted 'Thy will' to include what it did.

By the time the Baptists and the Methodists had raced each other to the local Mexican restaurant, two members of the town's football team were dead. Tyler 'T-Pain' Jones went into organ failure early Sunday morning, and his good friend and running back Sam Kristakis followed a few hours later. Coach Grizz was still hanging on, but he had been downgraded from serious to critical condition. Two more boys were also in bad shape, and another ten had milder symptoms.

Dr. Rowe, for his part, was at a loss about what else he could do. The small hospital's supply of antibiotics was nearly exhausted, and he already had to call some of Philadelphia's more advanced treatment centers to find the higher level antibiotics that his patients now needed. The first and second-line drugs weren't strong enough, and medicines of last resort like Carbapenems weren't easy to find in small towns like Halliston.

Frustrated and out of other options, Dr. Rowe went in search of Bill Davis. *I need to find out what happened at that practice.*

The Chief of Surgery found the football coach sitting in the waiting room with the players and staff who weren't sick. Pulling Coach Davis aside, Rowe began with his questions.

"What happened at practice? Give me the play-by-play."

"Okay," the coach nodded. "The boys all showed up around 8:30am. We wanted to get in a good practice before it got too hot. They ran a couple of laps, stretched, and then we started in on agility stations. Footwork ladders, pushing sleds, that kind of thing."

"And everything seemed fine?"

"Yeah, nothing out of the ordinary. We gave them a water break after about thirty minutes, started doing drills again, another water break at the hour mark, and then about an hour and fifteen minutes into practice the boys started puking everywhere."

"Speaking of water," Dr. Rowe asked, "has the team - or maybe even just the ones who got sick - gone on any swimming trips recently? You know, 'let's go rafting and bond for the upcoming season' or anything like that?"

Coach Davis shook his head. "Not that I know of. Plus, even if they had, Coach Grizz wouldn't have gone with them."

"No, I guess he wouldn't have." Dr. Rowe decided to level with the man sitting in front of him. "Look, what we're dealing with is a type of illness that destroys tissue in the body. I can't call it necrotizing fasciitis because they all tested negative for that, but every symptom points to something in that disease family."

"English please?" asked the coach.

"A flesh-eating bacteria," Dr. Rowe replied.

"Holy shit."

"Yeah, I know. And what has my staff and me so frustrated is that we can't figure out how so many people were exposed to it at the same time. That's why I asked about the swimming. If they had all been in the same river or lake recently that might explain things."

"What about drinking the same water?" Davis said.

"What do you mean?"

"We make the boys all drink out of a hose at practice." The coach grimaced. "Part of my old school charm."

Things started to connect in Chief Rowe's mind. "The ones who are sick . . . they drank from the hose?"

Davis nodded, guilt creeping into his eyes. "The sickest ones are all seniors, so they would've been the first in line. I was drinking Gatorade, but I think Grizz forgot his water bottle yesterday so he used the hose too."

Dr. Rowe patted the man on his shoulder. "Thanks Coach. This helps."

****

News outlets in the greater Philadelphia area had run a few segments about the sick football players on Saturday night, but the story exploded on Sunday when the boys started dying. Reporters flooded the small town of Halliston, and extra police were sent over from nearby areas to help with crowd control. In the era of internet and twenty-four hour cable news channels, people couldn't seem to get enough details about the All-American town suffering from an unexplained tragedy.

One person watching the news closely was Joseph Carlson. Sitting on the living room couch in his affluent suburban home, Dr. Carlson was far removed from the immediate troubles in Halliston, yet also intimately connected to them.

He repeated the words of the television reporter: "four dead, one more in critical condition, and ten hospitalized with milder yet still serious symptoms."

Joseph should have been happy. The bacteria was working. *But it's not working how I wanted it to*, he thought. The doctor stood up from his couch and walked into his kitchen. *Back to the drawing board*, Joseph thought as he unlocked the hidden door and descended the ladder into his secret lab. TV commentators spoke of how sad it was that all of the people in Halliston who got the illness had either died or were quickly on their way, but Dr. Carlson wasn't satisfied.

"They aren't dying quickly enough," Joseph said. He walked over to a worktable covered in test tubes, microscopes, and other research materials. "I need them dying faster. The longer they stay alive the better the chance that the antibiotics will kick in and they'll recover." He huffed his disapproval. "Recovery is not an option."

Joseph sat on a stool and closed his eyes, trying to remember every step in the process when he made his first bacteria drop. *The number of infected people is higher than we expected, but they're not as sick as we want.* "That means it's too diluted in the water," he said. "Okay. We can fix that. I just have to find a way to make it more concentrated. I need something to bond to the bacteria so that the water won't cause it to disperse so much."

Joseph opened his eyes. "But that still won't be enough. I need the bacteria itself to be stronger. More deadly."

Dr. Carlson spun around on the stool, stood up, and went back upstairs to his kitchen in search of coffee. "It's going to be a long week," he announced to the empty room. "Work during the day and then retrofitting the bacteria at night." He took a long sip from his mug. "Better get started."

EIGHTEEN

When Sunday night rolled into Monday morning, Dr. Carlson reluctantly put his new research on hold and went to work at the NIH. After all, he had to keep up appearances.

In nearby Washington, DC, members of President Richard Hughes' senior staff were busy starting up yet another workweek. Busiest among them was Daniel Bader, the Chief of Staff. Just as he was about to call a Senator to discuss an upcoming bill, the president's voice rang through his deputy's office.

"Danny!"

The Chief of Staff cringed. Daniel Bader knew that his boss was particularly upset when he called him Danny. Usually, it was 'Daniel' or 'Bader' or 'hey you.' When President Hughes called him Danny, something was going on.

"What is it, sir?" Bader responded, walking into the Oval Office from his workspace in the adjoining room. It wasn't that Daniel didn't know about the various issues and problems that the West Wing staff would be addressing that day. He was Chief of Staff - it was his job to know about them all. No, his question was more a matter of figuring out *which* problem the president was referring to this time.

A visibly frustrated Richard Hughes stood up from his desk and began to pace the floor. "I understand," he began, gesturing widely with his hands, "that each president has his defining thing. Lincoln had the Civil War. Reagan had the Cold War. George W. Bush had 9/11." Hughes paused to take a deep breath. "How the hell - seriously - how the hell did I end up being the viral outbreak president? Of all things, I get this. Seriously."

So that's what we're talking about, Daniel Bader thought. *The sick people in Pennsylvania.* "Well, sir, it's not really something that's within your control."

Bader's friend since college and best man at his wedding glared back at him. Richard didn't often pull rank while the two men were alone, but Daniel could tell this was going to be one of those times. "Wrong answer, Danny. Fix it. Find out what made those people sick, and fix it. I will not have another SuperAIDS on my hands. That *will not* be my legacy."

"Yes sir," the Chief of Staff responded with a nod. "I'm on it."

****

Down the street from the White House, the buzz around FBI Headquarters was also centered on the weekend's events in Pennsylvania. "What do you think caused it?" "I heard the Philadelphia field office has taken over the investigation." "I wonder if they'll send anyone from Headquarters up there."

Just about the only person not huddled around a water cooler discussing the case was Agent Reagan White. The twelve-year Bureau veteran had enough work on her hands without trying to play armchair quarterback on a case that was probably nothing more than a random mishap or a bunch of teenagers thinking it would be cool to eat wild mushrooms.

Reagan was in her office reviewing witness interview reports from an unsolved murder when she heard a familiar bellowing sound:

"Agent White!"

The thirty or so other agents and staff on the twelfth floor of the FBI headquarters simply rolled their eyes and continued working, ignoring the yelling from one end of the floor to the other. They were all used to it by now. Many had tried to convince the yeller, their boss, of the virtues of telephones, emails, and inner-office instant-messaging. Many had tried, and all had failed. So the Assistant Deputy Director's yelling was accepted as part and parcel of the workday. If he called your name, you went to his office. If he didn't, you ignored it.

"Agent White!" ADD Molina bellowed again. "My office! Now!"

A great many of the younger agents and staff admired the way that Reagan took her time while crossing from her corner office to that of her boss, located on the exact opposite end of the floor. Admired it: yes. Imitated it: no. Agent White had earned her stripes long ago and many times over. She could afford to keep Bruce Molina waiting. Very few other people could.

"What the hell took you so long?" Molina barked when Reagan strolled through his office door. In real time, no more than two minutes had passed. But two minutes was a lifetime in the ADD's book.

"I was reading a file and didn't want to lose my train of thought," the tall, slender woman responded casually. After twelve years of working for the FBI, five of which were spent reporting directly to the man in front of her, there was little that fazed Agent White anymore.

"Shut the door, White. And take a seat," Molina ordered, gesturing to the chairs positioned across the desk from him.

The thirty-four year old agent did as she was told, all the while fighting to suppress the urge to roll her eyes at her boss. Her caseload truly was ridiculous at the moment, and Bruce Molina never seemed to understand that she wasn't Superwoman and couldn't be in five places at the same time.

"What is it?" Reagan asked impatiently.

Bruce Molina's face was grim as he replied: "I'm sure you've heard about the high school football team from the town north of Philadelphia who all caught that flesh-eating disease."

Reagan made no effort to hide her response to the phrase 'flesh-eating.' "Yes sir, I heard about it on the news."

Her boss nodded his head. "Good. Then I'll skip the rather gruesome particulars. Bottom line: doctors up there are telling our local field agents that this isn't like any other bacteria they've dealt with before. It acts the same but it's not the same." Molina shook his head. "I don't know. I'm not a doctor. But I just got off the phone with the Director, who in turn had just talked to the President's Chief of Staff. They're concerned that this might have been a deliberate poisoning." The white-haired, Clint Eastwood lookalike reached for a folder on his desk as he continued talking. "You worked on that viral outbreak a couple of years ago, so this one is yours too."

Reagan sighed and nodded her head in understanding as she accepted the file. "Yes sir."

When Agent White stood up to leave, her boss joined her. His voice was as serious as she had ever heard it before. "People up there are dropping like flies, White. Get to the bottom of this. Fast."

Again Reagan nodded her head, her strawberry blonde ponytail bouncing up and down as she did. "Yes sir," she repeated. "I'll do my best."

NINETEEN

"When they said I would be working with the Bureau's best field agent, I didn't expect you to be so young. Or a girl."

The stranger's voice and condescending words caused Reagan's head to snap up from the folder she had been reading. "Excuse me?" she replied, more than a little irritated that a stranger was waiting for her in her office when she got back from meeting with her boss.

The tall, athletic man with brown hair and milk chocolate eyes put his hands up defensively even as he sat down on the edge of Reagan's desk. "Don't get me wrong: it was a compliment."

"A backhanded one," Reagan snorted.

"Yeah, okay, I'll grant you that much," the man replied with a grin.

There are a lot of cocky, chauvinistic people working in the FBI, but this one just might take the cake, thought Agent White. "I'm sorry," she said, "but who are you? And why are you in my office?"

Reagan hadn't ever been the type to get flustered over a guy, but she couldn't help but notice the quick flash of butterflies in her stomach when her rather handsome visitor laughed and stood up from her desk to walk toward her. Extending his hand in greeting, the man said: "Agent Allen Williams, Counterterrorism. ADD Molina told me I'd be working with you on the new flesh-eating bacteria case."

Reagan shook Agent Williams' hand, albeit warily.

"You don't look like you believe me," Allen stated as he helped himself to a chair.

"Because I don't. I've been with the Bureau for twelve years now and I've never heard of you. Plus the Assistant Deputy Director didn't say anything to me about having a partner on this case."

At that very moment, much to Agent White's chagrin, her boss poked his head around the corner of her still-open office door.

"Oh, good. You're already here," Molina said, nodding in Allen's direction. Looking over to Reagan, he added: "Agent Williams is going to partner up with you on the Pennsylvania thing. He's kind of our counterterrorism guru, so you two should complement each other well."

****

Allen smiled and nodded in response to his new supervisor's endorsement. "I'm sure we will," he said confidently. Agent Williams knew that confidence had been and would continue to be key to his success at the Bureau. It was one of two traits mentioned in all of his performance reviews: 'displays excellent confidence' right next to some version of 'does superb work.'

The thirty-five year old Virginia native had always received high marks at work and in school. Born and raised in the tony DC suburb of McLean, the older of two children had Type-A written all over him. He was also very close with his younger sister and made friends easily, leading Allen to be one of the 'cool kids' wherever he went. When he was honest with himself, though, Agent Williams knew that a lot of the gregariousness was for show. At his core, Allen was a nerd . . . he just hid it well. The boy voted Most Outgoing by his senior high classmates actually better fit the mold of 'too school for cool'. But his high-powered lobbyist father wouldn't stand for having a dorky son, so Allen learned to mask his love for numbers by channeling it into sports. *Knowing my game stats helps me be a better player*, he would argue. Or: *it makes the games so much more interesting if you keep track of the numbers. It's moneyball, Dad. Everybody does it.*

But Allen knew that nerdy wouldn't play well in this current situation. Smart: yes. Dorky: no. Agent Williams was known around the Bureau as a guy's guy, a bro, a throwback to a bygone era of G-Men. So he rose from his chair to shake hands with his new boss and flashed a cocky half-grin when the Assistant Deputy Director left the room. Turning around to face his partner, Allen immediately took the lead.

"What are we waiting for? Let's get started."

****

Later that evening, after an exhausting day of reshuffling her caseload and literally and figuratively bumping into Allen Williams in her office, Reagan returned to her fourth-floor walk-up to relax and try to get some actual work done. As usual, Agent White's first action upon returning home was to change out of her uncomfortable, off-the-rack black suit and into sweatpants and a t-shirt.

"Okay, Ari," Agent White said as she rubbed her pet cat on the head and opened her laptop on the coffee table in front of her. Crossing her feet under her legs, Reagan said, "let's do a little bit of research, yeah? If I'm going to be figuring out who is poisoning people then I need to know how this illness works."

Reagan much preferred this work environment to the one she experienced that day at FBI Headquarters. As an only child, Agent White grew up alone and didn't like working with other people. Group projects in school were her worst nightmare. Oftentimes, as a young student, Reagan would offer to do all of the work for her group and let everyone take credit as if it was a joint accomplishment. That way she wouldn't have to interact with the group and she would know all of the work was done properly. *It's just easier that way*, she thought. In that regard, Agent White was much like the man she was tasked with finding: both Reagan and Joseph were loners. They grew up alone and preferred to live their lives alone. But unlike the killer doctor, Reagan knew she was deeply loved. Her parents adored her, but more in the way that grandparents adore grandchildren. Her father was forty-eight and her mother forty-one when their miracle baby was born, and no matter how hard they tried there was always a bit of disconnect. A generational gap.

Reagan hadn't spoken to her parents in almost a month, but she knew that dwelling on that fractured relationship wouldn't be of any help with her current assignment. Shaking off the personal matters and skimming through the case file that she had placed in her lap, Reagan quickly found the name of the bacteria that the patients in Pennsylvania all tested positive for: necrotizing fasciitis. Well, technically the file said 'presents similar to, but fails test for, necrotizing fasciitis.' Agent White leaned forward and typed the medical term into her Google search engine.

"Eww!"

Reagan immediately X-ed out of her internet browser. Along with links to Wikipedia, WebMD, and the CDC's websites, Reagan's search also presented her with actual photos of infected patients. And there was no way she was going to look at those pictures any more than she already had. "They aren't kidding with that 'flesh-eating' part. Blehhhh."

"Yuck yuck yuck!" Reagan declared. "That's gross, Ari!"

The cat, for his part, simply stretched and yawned, obviously not happy at having been woken up by his owner's outburst.

Taking a deep breath, Reagan stared back at her computer screen. *Get it together, White*, she thought. *Stop being such a girl. You've seen mutilated bodies before. This is research. This is important.* Using one of her father's favorite phrases, Reagan muttered: "get on it, daggonit."

Luckily, her eyes and stomach were spared by the sound of a knock on her apartment door.

The knock startled Reagan. Other people living in the building weren't known for being very neighborly, and if anyone else had come to see her they would've had to buzz up to her apartment first.

Ari darted into Reagan's bedroom to hide. *So much for having a guard cat*, Reagan mused.

The agent walked steadily but cautiously to her front door, standing to the side and craning her neck over so she could see out the peep hole. Reagan didn't really think she had any reason to be worried, but as an FBI agent who had arrested hundreds people in her career, she was naturally extra cautious.

Her self-imposed caution, at least this time, was unnecessary. Reagan expelled the breath that she hadn't realized she was holding and went to work unlocking and unlatching her door. Swinging it open, she stared in confusion at the man standing in front of her, his hands carrying what looked like bags of takeout food.

"What are you doing here?" Reagan asked.

Allen Williams grinned. "Nice to see you too. I've got Indian and Chinese," he added, lifting up each bag as he referenced it. "I didn't know which one you would prefer, so I brought both."

Reagan continued to stare at her new work partner. She had never had a partner before, not in twelve years with the Bureau, and she didn't know why her boss thought she needed one now. Especially a partner like this Agent Williams character. A Vineyard Vines and boat shoes wearing man whose job it was to think of ways that criminals could kill people.

"Well?" Allen asked a little impatiently. "Can I come in?"

Reagan shifted her weight from one foot to the other and crossed her arms under her chest. "I don't know, can you?"

Allen issued a half-laugh, half-snort in response. "I should know better." He smiled. "*May* I come in, please?"

"Yeah, sure, I guess. I'm sorry the apartment is such a mess."

Allen looked around the nearly spotless kitchen where he now stood and wondered what Agent White was talking about. "Looks clean to me," he said, taking paper tins out of plastic bags and placing them on the table. "It's a lot cleaner than my apartment that's for sure."

He smiled again with that last sentence and couldn't help but notice that Reagan reacted to his smile with a frown. *She clearly doesn't like me*, Allen thought. *I guess my idea of a dinner bribe didn't work.*

"You still haven't answered my question," Reagan said, her harsh tone cutting through Allen's thoughts.

"And what question would that be?"

"Why are you here?"

By this point, Agent Williams was starting to get annoyed by his new partner's rude attitude. "What, you mean you haven't figured it out yet? You, Reagan White, investigator extraordinaire?" he replied, his voice dripping with sarcasm.

"Obviously not," Reagan shot back. "And I don't really appreciate you barging into my home unannounced." Reagan took a deep breath as if to reload, and then fired again: "just how exactly did you get into my building anyway? Breaking and entering is frowned upon, you know. Even for FBI agents."

Williams realized that he had overshot his target. His aim hadn't been to upset Reagan - he only wanted to show her that he could hold his own. Allen actually really liked his new partner; he knew her work by reputation, of course, and her feisty attitude meant there weren't likely to be many dull moments during this assignment.

"Look, I'm sorry," Allen began, switching tactics. "I didn't break in. Someone who lives in the building was walking in ahead of me, saw that my hands were full with the food, and held the door open for me. Not exactly a safe thing to do, but certainly not a crime."

When he saw that Reagan appeared to accept his explanation, Allen continued: "I came over tonight because I thought it would be good to go ahead and keep working on our investigation. Whoever is behind this water poisoning is already way ahead of us. And I brought dinner," he added, "because I'm hungry and I thought you might be too."

"Oh," Reagan replied. She dropped her arms to her sides and her eyes to the floor in embarrassment. Looking back up at Allen, she said: "well, I guess that all makes sense. Here, let me get us some plates for the food and then we can get started."

****

Reagan took a bite of her dinner and stared at her new partner. The two agents had cleared her table and were now seated in the kitchen, surrounded by takeout food and their laptops.

"I've read your file," Agent White confessed. "What's a blue blood like you doing working for the FBI?"

"Huh?"

"Oh come on," Reagan replied. "Born and raised in McLean? Georgetown Prep followed by Georgetown University? Excuse me, *cum laude* from Georgetown University? Your dad is a founding partner at one of DC's most powerful lobbying firms. Why aren't you doing something like that? Making millions and changing the course of history?"

"Well," Allen said slowly, "first of all, I do believe I'm changing the course of history. Saving lives and preventing terrorist attacks is monumental work. And as for the rest of it . . . you sound like my dad. He always asks me when I'm going to quit playing police officer and join his firm. But I don't want his life. I like mine just fine, thank you very much."

Reagan paused. *Touchy subject. Fine, moving on.* "Okay then, Mr. Preventing Terrorism Expert, where do suggest we begin?"

Reagan knew she still sounded a bit snarky, but she didn't care. Bruce Molina had trusted her to investigate SuperAIDS by herself . . . she didn't need any handholding from mister preppy fraternity member out of the Joint Terrorism Task Force.

Mr. Preppy just smiled and opened a container of Chinese food, not even making an attempt with the chopsticks before diving in with his fork. "Well," he said between bites, "you're actually the investigations expert. I just sit in a room and play 'if I were a terrorist' all day."

Allen started to laugh but stopped when he saw Reagan wasn't interested in funny. *Tough crowd*, he thought.

Reinforcing that thought, Reagan asked the question that had been on her mind all day: "then why are you here?"

Agent Williams leaned back against his chair, a look of confusion laced with hurt on his face. "I don't understand."

"You don't understand what?"

"I only met you a couple of hours ago. What could I have possibly done to make you not like me?"

Reagan didn't back down, not even in the face of the seriously adorable puppy dog eyes that Allen was throwing out at her. "I've been a field agent for twelve years," she said. "I've never needed a partner before. I don't need one now."

Allen nodded. "I get it. I'm not exactly thrilled to be partnered up either. I usually work alone."

"Could've fooled me," Reagan shot back.

"Look, we're stuck working together whether we like it or not. I figure I might as well try to embrace it as a new challenge and a new adventure. There's no use getting worked up and being miserable about it all the time."

Reagan thought for a minute then sighed. "I guess you're right. Just don't get offended if at some point I forget you exist and go off doing my own thing."

A deep male laughter filled Reagan's apartment, a sound so rare that even Ari the cat poked his head around the corner to see what was going on. *Man, he's got a great laugh,* Reagan thought before catching herself and shaking her head clear.

"I won't get offended," Allen promised. "Now you tell me, investigator: where do we start?"

TWENTY

"Most of what we need to do is pretty basic," Reagan said. "You'll remember it from the Academy."

"Speaking of the Academy," Williams interrupted, "Have you heard about any new leads on that instructor who went missing?"

Reagan held up a finger telling Allen to wait while she finished chewing her food. "No," she finally replied. "Baltimore and Metro PD have assisted us in the search, but last I heard the trail went cold."

"That's so bizarre."

A silence fell over the room as both FBI agents thought back to their Academy instructors and how it easily could've been one of them who disappeared.

Agent Williams snapped back to the present. "Sorry to interrupt. I was just curious. Please, continue: 'it's all pretty basic . . .'"

"Yep," Reagan nodded, putting her carton of sweet and sour chicken to the side to make room for her laptop. She was eternally grateful to whomever gave the go-ahead for case files to be digitized, if for no other reason than she didn't have to lug them up four flights of stairs to her apartment anymore.

"I've already called and talked to the agents on the ground in Pennsylvania as well as the Centers for Disease Control. They've confirmed that the disease is some version of flesh-eating bacteria and that the people got it through drinking contaminated water."

Allen glanced down at the plate in front of him. "Maybe we don't talk about the disease itself until after we're finished with dinner."

Reagan looked at her own food as well and nodded. "Yeah, good idea."

"Okay," she said, "so we know it's connected somehow to the town's water supply. Witnesses said the football players and coaches were all drinking water from a hose at practice and then started getting sick. First thing we need to do is make a list of everyone who has access to the water treatment plant and see if any of them throw up any red flags."

"Right, of course," Allen said. "It's like Academy hypos. Make the list, check for prior arrests or investigations, then cross that with people who might have had a reason to poison the water."

"Means, motive, and opportunity," Reagan simplified.

Allen nodded. "It seems to me that the first thing we should actually do is hop in a car and drive up there to Halliston. What is it from here, like three or four hours? Let's see it all first hand."

This time it was Reagan's turn to smile. "You really don't spend much time in the field, do you?"

"No. Why?"

"Budget cuts," she explained. "If we want to travel to Pennsylvania, we'll have to get approval from Molina first."

"Okay, so let's get approval. I highly doubt they'll turn us down for an investigation like this. And in the meantime," Allen reasoned, picking up his mushroom masala, "we can eat dinner and work on our list of possible suspects."

****

Reagan arrived at work the next morning to find her new partner waiting for her. *Overachiever*, she thought.

Allen began speaking before Reagan even had a chance to put down her briefcase. "Mornin', partner!" he said in a fake country accent.

Agent White rolled her eyes. "G'morning," she mumbled.

"Uh oh, somebody's not a morning person."

Reagan walked back around her desk and out of her office, heading in the direction of coffee in the break room. "I do fine in the mornings," she replied. "I just need some coffee first."

"Well, make it a cup to go," Allen said.

Reagan stopped walking and whirled around to face her partner. "Why?"

Agent Williams grinned. "I talked to Molina. We're cleared to travel up to Pennsylvania."

"You what?"

"I talked to Bruce. He said we should absolutely travel up to Halliston and check things out."

Reagan was shocked. "You talked to *Bruce?*"

"Yeah. We're on a first name basis over in CTR - that's counterterrorism research - so I asked the Assistant Deputy Director if he minded." Allen shrugged. "Promotes team bonding, don't you think?"

Reagan snorted. "No. I don't think." She turned back around and resumed her coffee run. "Look, I'm glad we got approval to go up to Halliston. Just don't be thinking you can come in here and change everything. I'm the agent with field experience. I'm in charge of the investigation."

Much to her consternation, Allen was visibly amused by Reagan's tough girl attitude. Standing at attention, he saluted her. "Yes ma'am." Then, with yet another grin, he added: "now get that coffee so we can get on the road. I'll drive."

****

An hour and a half into their drive from Washington, DC to Halliston, Pennsylvania, Reagan's ears had had enough.

"Do you ever stop talking?" she said.

Allen, who was driving the car, turned his head sideways and shrugged his shoulders. "I'm just trying to help pass the time."

"That's what the radio is for."

"Oh come on, White. Relax. Let your hair down a little bit."

Reagan reflexively reached behind her head and pulled her ponytail tighter.

Allen laughed, the same deep masculine laugh that filled her apartment the night before. "Seriously," he said. "Don't you ever just chill? Go out . . . have a good time?" He paused. "What do you say, when this is all over you and me have dinner together?"

"We ate dinner together last night."

Agent Williams sighed. "I don't mean take-out food at your apartment. Like dinner dinner; you know, dress up, pick a restaurant, see where the evening takes us?"

Reagan folded her arms across her chest and stared at the road straight ahead. "I don't date work colleagues."

"Ever?"

She nodded. "Ever. I want to keep my personal and professional lives separate."

"Alright," a rejected Allen replied. "I can respect that." He grinned. "I might still try to change your mind, but I can respect that. How about a new topic, okay? What road game do you want to play? Counting cars? Cows?"

"Cows?"

"Yeah. Whenever we drive past cows, the first person to say 'cows' gets to claim that bunch. You can claim other related stuff too, like other farm animals, hay for your horses, etcetera."

"So you just keep calling out cows?"

"Mmm hmm. The really fun part is if you pass a cemetery. The first person to call that gets to kill the other person's cows."

"That's horrible!"

Agent Williams laughed again. "The cows don't actually die."

Reagan folded her arms across her chest. "I know that. I still think it's horrible."

"Okay then," Allen said. "No cows game. I have a better idea anyway. I don't know anything about you. Tell me ten things that you think I should know."

"Ten?"

Allen shrugged his shoulders. "It's a long drive. And that's not that many."

Reagan looked at her new partner skeptically. "You used to get 'talks too much' on your report cards in school, didn't you?"

"Only once," he admitted. "My dad spanked me so hard that I never acted up in class again. But quit changing the subject. Ten things. Go."

Agent White leaned back in her seat in the car and tried to think of what to say. Nobody had ever asked her something like this before. The quiet, gangly, pimply daughter of an accountant and a schoolteacher didn't have many friends growing up, and Reagan much preferred the company of a good book over playing with any of the children in her neighborhood. So this, now? This ten fact challenge? *It will probably be the longest I've ever talked about myself.*

Beside her, Allen felt Reagan's hesitation. "I'll help you get started," he said. "Where did you grow up?"

Reagan relaxed a little bit. *Easy question.* "I grew up in Tampa, Florida. That's one thing. I'm an only child," she added. "That's two."

Agent White paused to think. "I went to Central Florida for college and studied Criminology. Three and four."

"Why'd you decide to become an FBI agent?" Agent Williams asked.

Reagan paused again, trying to decide whether or not to tell the truth. "Do you promise you won't laugh?"

Allen nodded his head yes.

"The movie 'Miss Congeniality.'"

Agent Williams pressed his lips together in an effort to disguise his amusement.

"Go ahead. Laugh. I know it's a dumb reason."

Allen's smile diminished. "It's not a dumb reason at all. It's just not one I've heard before."

"Well I always wanted to do some form of law enforcement work," she explained, "and when I saw that movie I thought 'hey, why not FBI?'"

"And here you are," said Allen.

Reagan nodded. "Here I am. That's five, by the way."

"I know. Keep going."

"Okay. Six: I named my cat Aristotle after the philosopher because he was one of the favorites of my favorite college professor. Seven: I hate Thai food. Like seriously can't stand it."

"Duly noted," Allen said.

"Eight: my favorite color is purple. And I liked purple before Justin Bieber was even born so don't you dare try to make that connection."

Her partner laughed again. "Okay, yes to purple, no to Bieber references. You've got two more."

"My favorite movie is 'My Best Friend's Wedding' and my favorite ice cream is chocolate chip cookie dough." Reagan relaxed back further into her seat. "Your turn, chatterbox."

Allen took an exaggerated breath and cracked his knuckles as if he was warming up for an event. "Okay, here goes. I grew up in McLean, Virginia, just outside of DC. I have a younger sister who is a book agent in Raleigh. I went to Georgetown for college and majored in American Studies with a minor in Arabic. A useless major and a terrorist minor, in my dad's opinion."

Reagan sensed a note of hostility between Allen and his father, but she didn't say anything.

"What's next? Oh yeah, why I became an FBI agent. I was recruited by several three-letter agencies coming out of college, but I didn't like the secrecy that a lot of them entailed. The man who was my supervisor before this case came to campus one day and told me about the counterterrorism research division of the Bureau, and from that day on I knew what I wanted to do."

Reagan smiled. "A much better answer than 'I watched Miss Congeniality.'"

Allen shook his head. "Nah, yours is better. Much more fun." He paused. "Let's see, five more. I don't have a cat named Aristotle. I don't have any pets. I would love to get a dog but I'm not home enough to take care of it."

"Cats are a lot easier," said Reagan.

"Yeah, but I'm selfish. If I'm going to feed and house an animal, I want it to overtly display its unconditional love and affection for me. Cats are too moody."

Reagan huffed her disapproval, and Allen quickly backtracked. "Too moody for my taste. Like I said, I'm selfish. Aristotle seemed very nice."

His partner let Williams suffer for a few seconds before nodding her head in acceptance of his apology. "Continue," she said.

"I love Thai food but I will not eat sushi. I want my meat cooked, thank you very much. My favorite color is blue. I know," he said, "standard male answer. My favorite movie is a trilogy. 'The Godfather'. Although Part III really wasn't all that great. And," Allen said with a deep breath, "number ten, last but not least, my favorite ice cream is moose tracks."

Reagan nodded. "Good choice."

A silence descended on the agents' car. *I can't believe it*, Reagan thought. *He finally ran out of things to say.*

TWENTY-ONE

"Hey, what about this guy?"

"What guy?" Allen asked. He and Reagan were huddled in little more than an emptied-out broom closet at the Halliston Sheriff's Office and looking at a list of possible poisoning suspects. The two were sitting in plastic chairs borrowed from the high school, with their shared pizza resting on an upside down crate.

"Him," Reagan answered, passing over a list of names. "Jonathan Banks."

Agent Williams scanned the list to find the person his partner referenced. "Jonathan Banks, twenty-six, moved here five years ago to work for the city utilities department." Allen paused. "He had opportunity, sure, but what motive? He still works there; nobody had any complaints about him."

"Two things," Reagan said, sitting up straighter in her chair and folding her long legs up under her body.

She can't sit still when she gets excited, a bemused Allen noticed. *She's like a kid on her way to the candy store.*

"Number one," Reagan went on, unaware of Allen's thoughts, "he's the only person who had access to the water supply who isn't from this town."

"So?"

"So . . . everybody else would have been putting family and friends at risk. Jonathan Banks didn't have to worry about that."

Agent Williams wasn't convinced. "Surely, after living here for five years, the guy made some friends."

"Nuh uh," Reagan said, shaking her head back and forth as she reached for another slice of pizza. "His profile says he's a loner."

"Okay. What else? You said there are two things."

"He was $75,000 in debt."

"Was or is?" Allen asked.

"Was," Agent White replied with a grin, a cat-caught-the-canary gleam in her eyes. "His financial records show that the debt was paid in full on Monday."

"Okay then. Let's go pick him up."

****

Jonathan Banks lived on the outskirts of Halliston in a duplex near the old steel mill. The siding on the house was yellowing and starting to rot, and Reagan swore she could smell mold even while standing on Banks' front porch.

"Try to let me do most of the talking, alright?" Agent White said to her partner. "I know you've been an agent for a long time, but this is your first assignment in the field."

Allen nodded reluctantly. "Okay. I'll try." He turned his head and gave Reagan an impish grin. "Can't make any promises though."

Reagan rolled her eyes. "And quit smiling. This is a murder investigation."

A car pulled into the driveway and caused the two agents to stop talking. A tall, slightly overweight man fitting Jonathan Banks' description exited the old Chevy and started walking toward the front door.

"Can I help you?" he asked, confusion mixing with bravado.

Reagan pulled out her badge. "I'm Agent Wh - "

Before she could finish the sentence, Banks turned around and bolted down the driveway, past his car and into the residential street.

Shit, thought Allen. *Why do they always run?* He then took off after the suspect, using the speed that served him well in high school sports to chase down the out-of-shape Banks.

Agent Williams caught up to the utilities man five houses down the street, launching into the air to tackle him from behind. Allen was struggling to keep the larger man on the ground when Reagan arrived with handcuffs. Service weapon drawn, a steely-eyed Agent White made sure Jonathan Banks didn't move while her partner got him handcuffed and back on his feet.

The three then walked down the road to Allen's car, climbed in, and drove in the direction of the Sheriff's station. *Time to make this punk spend a little time in the box*, Reagan thought.

****

'The box' was law enforcement code for the interrogation room. Halliston's Sheriff's Office had a small box in a back corner of the building, complete with speakers and a one-way mirror connected to an adjacent office. It was in that office where Agent Williams and the town's sheriff set up camp, watching while Reagan questioned Jonathan Banks.

"Since you didn't let me finish my sentence earlier," she began, "my name is Agent White. I'm with the FBI. The man who tackled you is my partner on this case, Agent Williams."

The handcuffed Banks offered no reply and continued to stare down at the table in front of him.

"Why did you run, Mr. Banks? Is it because you have something to hide?"

The suspect slowly raised his eyes to glare at Reagan. "No."

"No what?"

"No, I don't have anything to hide."

"Then why did you run?" Reagan pressed. "Innocent people don't usually run from the police."

Banks shrugged his shoulders. "Force of habit, I guess. Got in trouble a lot as a kid. Kinda became instinct: see a cop, run the opposite way."

Reagan nodded and scribbled 'check juvenile records' in her notebook. "Okay," she said. "I can believe that. Not everyone has a positive relationship with law enforcement. But that's really a habit you should break, Mr. Banks. Because now you're facing all kinds of fleeing the scene and resisting arrest charges."

His eyes shot back up. "What? Come on girl. I didn't do anything!"

Agent White pressed her lips together and took a deep breath. "To begin with, my name is not 'girl.' As I already told you, I am Agent White. You may call me 'Agent White.' Or 'ma'am.' But definitely not 'girl.'

"Fine. Sorry. *Agent White.*"

"Furthermore," Reagan continued, "if you cooperate with me here and answer my questions, I'll see what I can do about getting those charges dropped."

Banks sat up more in his metal chair and put his shackled hands on top of the table. "Okay. What do you want to know?"

Reagan wasted no time. "Monday morning when you woke up you were $75,000 in debt. By close of business you had paid the note in full. How?"

The man across the table from her was taken aback by White's direct approach. And her knowledge of his finances. "How'd you know that?"

"It's not a difficult thing to find out, Mr. Banks."

"Okay," he said. "Then it also shouldn't be too hard to find out that I won the scratch-off lottery on Saturday night. A hundred grand." Banks smirked at the FBI agent, knowing he had just blown a hole in her investigation. "I picked up the check first thing Monday morning and took it to the bank. Told them to use it to pay off my loan then put the rest in my savings account."

Reagan's stomach lurched but still she played it cool. "You know I'm going to check that story, right? And if any of it isn't true, I'll be adding false statements, obstruction of justice, and whatever else I can think of to your list of charges."

"It's true. Call the lottery office. They'll tell you."

Much to Reagan's chagrin, Jonathan Banks was telling the truth. A quick phone call to the Pennsylvania Lottery was all it took to destroy the FBI agents' first solid lead. Or what they thought had been a solid lead, anyway.

Reagan and Allen spent another twenty-four hours in Halliston, interviewing victims and witnesses and running into dead ends everywhere they turned. Frustrated and tired, the pair drove back down to DC on Thursday night to resume work from the FBI Headquarters.

TWENTY-TWO

The extensive news coverage of the flesh-eating bacterial outbreak in Pennsylvania told Joseph everything he needed to know when picking his next drop-off location. Namely, that it had to be in a completely different area of the country. So on the following Friday evening, the day after Allen and Reagan left Halliston, Dr. Carlson returned home from work, ate a quick dinner, and climbed back into his trusty silver sedan to head south - away from Halliston and away from Bethesda.

The second drop site wasn't hard to pick out. After only a few minutes of online research about water treatment plants in Georgia, Joseph had found a giant facility in the heart of downtown Atlanta. *It's amazing that no one has done this before*, Joseph thought. *Or maybe they have and just didn't do it correctly. Very possible, especially if they didn't have my level of expertise.*

Joseph arrived in the capital city of Georgia just after three a.m. and pulled his car into a large church parking lot about a mile away from the treatment plant. He wanted to make sure everything was completely prepared and ready to go before he drove anywhere near the actual site.

"We only get one shot at this," the doctor said, speaking to the array of materials that he was now assembling in his trunk. Two hours earlier, at a gas station in South Carolina, Dr. Carlson had begun the preparation process by putting pieces of specially-designed, absorbent yet dissolvable paper into petri dishes full of his bacteria. Now, in the parking lot, Joseph put on latex gloves and then pulled the dishes out of a cooler in his trunk. He also grabbed the small potato gun resting beside the cooler. Glancing over his shoulder several times, Joseph was happy to note that the parking lot was abandoned. *And it's not government property, so Big Brother with the spy cameras won't be able to see anything.*

Returning to the driver's seat of his car, Joseph gently placed the first of the bacteria-filled round dishes on the middle console of his car, lifting the top off and putting that in the passenger seat. He then slowly, carefully lifted a soaked piece of paper out of the dish, rolled it into a ball, and dropped it down the open end of the potato gun.

Thank you Keri Dupree for that idea, Joseph thought. *Since you wouldn't shut up about catching a t-shirt at the Nationals baseball game, it gave me the final answer I had been looking for: how to launch the bacteria over taller fences and into the water. The potato guns that they use to shoot prizes into the crowd at sporting events are perfect for the job. Even if it is a bit ridiculous. 'Keep it simple, stupid', right?*

That was Carlson's plan. The more advanced delivery mechanism he was going to use at his remaining treatment plant attacks. In Pennsylvania, Joseph had simply stepped over the chain at the entrance of the water facility, walked up to the edge of the retaining pond, and dumped a vial of bacteria into the water. Now, however, the doctor took strips of paper and soaked them in bacteria. At each drop location, he would load several pieces of paper into the t-shirt launcher. With his car window rolled down, Joseph could simply drive by the water treatment facility and launch the papers out of his car, across the road, over the fence, and into the water on the other side. No stopping and getting out of the car to manually chuck something over the fence. No trying to sneak past the guards to get closer access to the water. Just a man and his compressed-air gun. This way, Joseph would barely even have to slow down. And since he planned to do most - if not all - of the drops at night, there was little chance that anyone would notice projectiles flying out of the car in front of or behind them.

"Yep, it's official," Joseph said with a nod of his head and a smile. "I'm a genius."

****

The water treatment plant on Howell Mill Road in Atlanta wouldn't immediately strike passersby as a good target for a terrorist attack. Tall fences topped with razor wire surrounded the entire facility, and security cameras were placed strategically throughout the area. What stood out to Joseph, though, were the large open air ponds located immediately beside the road. He also noticed the heavy traffic, even in the middle of the night, and the relatively low numbers of street lights. *Perfect*, he thought.

As Joseph approached the plant, he rolled down his driver's side window and aimed the disease-laden potato gun in the direction of the treatment plant. Slowing his speed just slightly, the doctor pulled the trigger and watched as the small paper wads flew across the street, over the razor wire fence, and into the water on the other side.

"Jackpot!" Dr. Carlson said with a smile. He rolled up his window and continued on the road in the direction of the interstate and his next target.

TWENTY-THREE

On a stretch of US Highway 41, on the edge of what one could legitimately call metropolitan Atlanta, lied a small water treatment facility. Joseph's second target. The plant was off the road a little bit, up a small hill and surrounded by a high barbed-wire fence, which made it a less than ideal location for the drop. However, in this part of northern Georgia where the Appalachian Mountains began to rise and the exurbs fade into small town America, not many people were out on the road at 4am. In fact, Joseph saw no other cars from the time he exited the interstate to his arrival at the treatment plant.

About half a mile away from the facility, Joseph turned off the headlights on his car. Just as a precaution. The doctor drove with a purpose, pulling off the four-lane highway and on to a strip of asphalt that barely qualified as a road. Joseph drove his car as close to the fence as he could before shifting the gear into park. He glanced around the car, over to the brick building where the water was treated and back down the hill to the main road. "Get this over and done with," Joseph said. "This place gives me the creeps. It's too damn quiet."

Dr. Carlson's body did as it was told. Leaving the engine running, he quickly got out of the car and walked around to the trunk. There Joseph loaded three rounds of bacteria paper into the potato gun. The doctor's normally steady hands shook from nerves, the loud sounds of crickets filling the otherwise empty air.

"I don't know how anyone could live here," he muttered. "Too damn quiet."

The 'pop' from the potato gun's launch shot silenced even the crickets.

Knowing that at any moment the local sheriff could come driving by, Joseph quickly stashed his bacteria shooter back in the sealed cooler in his trunk, slammed it shut, and was back on Highway 41 seconds later. It wasn't until Joseph merged with the long-haul truckers and night owls on Interstate 75 that he finally allowed himself to breathe.

"No more small towns," he said. "And definitely no more small towns at night."

****

Joseph had learned many things during his first run of mass murdering, which he liked to call Operation Respect. He learned that doors to houses and secret labs must always stay closed and locked. That attention must be paid to details, from the big ones like which viral capsid to use all the way down to the small ones like which fake name and address to put on a donation form. He learned that he was a much better liar and actor than he thought he was.

And right then, driving along a stretch of road that was taking him north from his third attack site in Tennessee and back toward his home in Maryland, the doctor was putting into practice yet another lesson learned over the past several years: satellite radio is a gift from the music gods. Especially on long swaths of interstate home to signs like 'next exit: forty-five miles.'

In places like this, where the blacktop and the pine trees all seemed to meld together into an endless blur, Joseph Carlson was indescribably grateful to be able to listen to '80s rock instead of some country song about a man, a truck, beer, and Jesus.

Still another lesson learned came in the form of the case of energy drinks lying in the passenger side floorboard. All of this weekend's drops had been made - people in Atlanta, Emerson, Georgia, and Farragut, Tennessee were probably already getting sick. Now all Joseph had to do was make it back home in time to get enough sleep on Sunday so that

Keri wouldn't comment about how tired he looked on Monday.

Aluminum cans full of liquid speed and sing-along radio were just what Dr. Carlson needed. Lesson learned.

TWENTY-FOUR

"Yo, Asher, wake up."

Teddy Chandler kicked the side of the bed where his cousin was sleeping. The twenty-nine year old hung over houseguest simply moaned and rolled over.

"Seriously dude. You gotta wake up. We have to be at the club in an hour. Tee time is at 9:30 and my dad will be pissed if we're late."

"You're twenty-bloody-six years old," Asher's British accent mumbled into his pillow. "Your father can wait."

The man groaned again as he rolled onto his back and shielded his eyes from the early Saturday morning sunlight. "Tell him I'm tired from jet lag."

Teddy shook his head. "Wrong direction. It's early afternoon in London right now."

"Ahh bugger. Alright. I'm up. I'm up."

It took another few minutes before Asher's body got the message, though. He didn't go out partying often, but when he did he went hard. And now the vacationing bond trader was feeling the worst of last night's aftermath.

"How are you not wrecked like me?" Asher asked, making his way into his cousin's kitchen. It was a spacious two-bedroom loft condo in the West Midtown section of Atlanta, and was certainly nicer than anything he could afford in London. *Even if the building does overlook a water treatment plant*, Asher thought.

"I didn't drink as much as you," Teddy replied. Even though the two men grew up on different continents, they were close enough in age and personality that they had always been more like brothers than cousins.

"Here," the American said, handing his English counterpart a glass of water before picking up his own cup. "Drink this. We'll get you rehydrated and then switch to coffee for the drive over to the golf course."

Asher gave his cousin a wry smile. "You're a saint."

"I know." Teddy laughed. "Drink up. Seriously. I'm gonna go get changed. There are bagels and stuff on the counter if you're hungry."

Asher clutched his stomach and groaned. "Ugh, no. No food. Don't even talk about food."

A few minutes later, Teddy returned to the kitchen from his room. "Ready to go?"

He paused, confused.

"Ash, where are you?"

Teddy heard his cousin before he saw him. Heard the heaving convulsions and riotous vomiting coming from the guest bathroom. *Serves him right after drinking that much last night.*

Disregarding privacy, Teddy walked into the room and swung open the bathroom door. Lying on the floor, curled up in a fetal position, and drenched in his own vomit and feces, was Asher.

"Holy shit! Asher! Asher - talk to me! What happened?"

The man responded by hurling more bodily fluids onto his cousin's shoes.

"Dammit dude! What the hell did you drink last night?"

Asher was incapable of answering. He simply moaned in pain, interrupted only briefly by rounds of diarrhea and vomiting.

"Oh my God. Okay, Ash, just hang with me for a few more minutes. I'm gonna call an ambulance."

Running back into the kitchen, Teddy ignored the rumbling in his own stomach, quickly found his cell phone, and dialed 911.

"Hello? Yeah, I'm at 576 Peachtree Circle Way. Unit nine. I think my cousin has alcohol poisoning. Hurry!"

****

The drop off that scared Joseph the most, the one north of Atlanta with too much dark and too much quiet, was a place called Emerson. Place was indeed a more accurate label than town, since there was no proper town to speak of. Just country. A tiny little dot on a map. A drive-through between the suburbs of Atlanta and the towns of the north Georgia mountains, known more for its strict traffic law enforcement than anything else.

Two of Emerson's longtime residents, Fred and Janice Hart, appreciated the hard work of the police department in slowing down the fancy suburbanites who thought the speed limit was just a suggestion while on their way to the nearby lake.

The Harts liked where they lived for all of the reasons that Joseph hated it: peaceful, quiet. A place where not much ever happened and people were free to do and live as they pleased - provided their doing was honest work and their living involved worship every Sunday morning.

Several miles away from the hustle and bustle of the state park and the lake, Fred and Janice lived on a farm. Cattle, mostly, but also the occasional corn, hay, and pigs. Married for fifty-eight years, Janice knew that her seventy-six year old husband needed to stop working the farm and hire somebody else to do it. But the old man was as stubborn as his mule out in the barn. *Plus*, Janice thought while watching Fred from the kitchen window, *he wouldn't know what to do with himself if he ever stopped working. He'd be like Bear Bryant or Joe Paterno - the work was what kept them going. It's what keeps my Fred going too.*

Mrs. Hart let loose a long sigh and turned away from the window. She didn't like thinking about such things. "But at my age, what else do I have to think about?" The elderly woman never shied away from a little bit of morbid humor. *Keeps me young*, she thought, and laughed.

The grandfather clock in the front hall chimed eleven-thirty and Janice knew it was time to start making lunch. Fred would be in pretty soon and she didn't want him to have to wait to eat, even if it was only leftover meatloaf and pasta salad from the night before. Janice's mother had taught her how to cook the old-fashioned way, and as a result Mrs. Hart refused to reheat anything in the microwave. *It sucks out all of the flavor*, she thought.

The mother of four, grandmother of nine, and great-grandmother of two preheated the oven to 350-degrees before pulling the lunch containers out of the refrigerator. Feeling the warmth of the early summer Southern day streaming in through the kitchen windows, Janice poured herself a tall glass of water and sat down at the table while she waited for the oven to heat.

****

Twenty minutes later, Fred Hart emerged from the barn, drenched in sweat and smelling like the pigsty that he had spent the better part of the past hour cleaning.

The farmer wiped his forehead with his handkerchief and trudged toward his house and the lunch that he knew was waiting for him.

Fifty-eight years of marriage had housebroken Fred enough that he rinsed off his hands and face with the outside water hose and took off his boots in the mud room.

"What's for lunch?" he called out.

No reply.

That's strange, Fred thought.

"Janice, honey?" he said, walking into the kitchen.

Empty.

Even more strange.

Fred's next stop was down the home's main hall to the master bedroom.

"Jan? You in here?"

Mr. Hart was about to turn around to go check the other parts of the house when something on the floor of the bathroom caught his eye. He tried to open the door but was stopped halfway by a large object. Stepping in as far as he could, Fred saw what was blocking the door.

Janice.

Collapsed on the floor by the toilet, spewing vomit and diarrhea from all ends.

Janice, just barely conscious and unable to control whatever had caused her to be so violently ill, opened her eyes and lifted her head for just long enough to see her husband's face turn as white as a ghost.

"I'll . . . b-be . . . f-fine," she croaked.

Fred, however, wouldn't be. The elderly man clutched his left arm, groaned, and fell to the ground, overcome by the shock of seeing his wife so sick.

Twenty-four hours later, the Hart's neighbor stopped by to check on the couple. It was extremely rare for Fred and Janice to miss a Sunday morning at church. The concerned neighbor found them both lying on the floor in the bathroom, next to each other in death as they had been in life.

TWENTY-FIVE

"We begin our broadcast with an update on the rapidly developing story surrounding the recent outbreaks of flesh-eating bacteria. We have a full team investigating this and bringing you new information, starting with our reporter Page McDowell who is live for us in Atlanta tonight. Page, what's the latest?"

The camera cut to a bubbly blonde standing in front of a large white hospital building.

"Yes, good evening Tom. I'm here tonight at Grady Memorial Hospital in Atlanta where I'm told at least fourteen people are being treated for the same flesh-eating bacteria that struck Halliston, Pennsylvania last weekend. Doctors also confirmed that five people have now died at Grady from bacterial complications, although their identities are being withheld until the next of kin is notified. The number of deaths is expected to rise as the days go on."

"What about the investigation into the cause of the outbreak, Page?" the anchor interrupted. "Do you have any information on that?"

The reporter pressed her earpiece further into her ear to hear the question. "Yes Tom," she nodded, "I do. The Centers for Disease Control is headquartered here in Atlanta and they have people on site at Grady investigating. I was able to speak with one CDC official, a Dr. Gill Pingrey, who said it's too early to tell anything definitively but that this looks like it might be an intentional poisoning. Sobering news, Tom."

The anchor nodded his head in agreement. "It certainly is, Page. Thank you. And now," he said, swinging his focus to a different camera, "we're going to take you live to Washington, DC and the White House for the Hughes Administration's reaction to this latest outbreak. Our Senior

White House Correspondent Hal Schneider has been on this story all day. Hal?"

****

"Have you heard the latest?" Caroline Simmons asked, the White House Deputy Chief of Staff making conversation with the Communications Director as they walked through the halls of the West Wing. The two advisors were on their way to a senior staff meeting with their boss, Daniel Bader.

"The latest on what?" her colleague asked. He dealt with dozens of different news topics every day, so figuring out what Caroline was referencing would be nearly impossible.

"The bad water. The flesh-eating bacteria thing." The woman cringed as she said the words 'flesh-eating.' It was a common reaction. Just the thought of one's body literally being eaten from the inside out was enough to make anyone squirm.

The Communications Director also cringed. "Ick. I think Daniel got it right when he said that the whole idea gave him the heebeegeebees."

The Deputy Chief of Staff nodded her head in agreement. They had arrived at the Chief of Staff's office and walked in unannounced, just in time to hear Daniel Bader say:

"...and now it appears that stores nationwide have sold out of home water filters."

"That's the latest," Caroline said quietly to the man next to her.

"Do those filters work?" another staffer asked.

"We don't know," Daniel Bader replied. "HHS and the CDC are testing them right now I think." He turned away from the window where he had been watching reporters make their evening broadcasts. "Even if they do work and can filter out this bacteria, we're still screwed. What are we supposed to do, set up distribution stations and give every household a free water filter?"

"I can see the backlash on that already," Caroline said. "Protests because of the cost. Tea Party groups picketing the White House - as if having your body eaten from the inside out by a killer bacteria is a patriotic duty."

"Let's not talk about the disease itself, okay?" asked the press secretary, making the same scrunched-up face of disgust that his colleague had earlier.

"You know I'm right though," the Deputy Chief of Staff continued. "Not to mention all of the government watchdogs screaming to see documentation on how we picked which filter to use and what that company's relationship is with the White House."

Their boss exhaled deeply, running his fingers through his thinning hair. "Let's hope it doesn't come to that. In the meantime, though, one of you get on the phone with the CDC or NIH or whoever is handling the medical stuff. Find out where we are on stopping this thing."

TWENTY-SIX

"Dammit!"

Allen Williams heard cussing coming from the twelfth floor conference room and quickly headed in that direction. Reagan didn't think swear words were appropriate for the office, so Allen knew she must be really upset.

"Reagan? You alright?"

Anger flashed in Agent White's eyes. "Do I look like I'm alright?"

The words slipped out of Agent Williams' mouth before he could stop them. "I think you look great, like you always do."

Reagan's hazel-colored eyes cut over to where Allen stood in the doorway, anger mixing with confusion and what resembled disdain. "I don't know how to respond to that," she said. "All I do know is that every investigative technique we would normally use - and have been using - has been blown to pieces by the outbreaks down in Georgia. I thought we were dealing with an isolated event: look for motive, look for opportunity, and we'll find him. But now we have multiple instances of probable terrorist attacks, across state lines, possibly using a chemical or biological agent."

"Damn," Allen responded.

"That's what I said." Reagan sighed. "All of the work we did in Pennsylvania is useless now. It's not as if we developed any solid leads there, but still . . . "

"Georgia is a game changer," Williams said, completing the thought.

Reagan nodded. "Definite game changer."

Allen stood up straight from where he had been leaning against the doorframe. "What are we waiting for, then? Let's get down there."

"Down to Georgia?"

"Yeah," Agent Williams said, already turning to walk toward their boss' office. Over his shoulder, he added: "and don't give me that crap about budgets and stingy trip approval. This is top priority. They're liable to fly us down there in a fricking jet."

****

Allen was right. He and Agent White did fly on one of the FBI's private planes, straight from a hanger at Reagan National Airport to a strip at Naval Air Station Atlanta and into an awaiting standard-issue, black FBI sedan.

This sure beats the rickety old rental car I had when investigating SuperAIDS a few years ago, Reagan thought. What came next to Reagan's mind wasn't pleasant.

"Hey Williams," she said.

"I told you, call me Allen. And hold on. I've got to get the address plugged into this GPS thing before we start driving."

A few seconds and several dozen punched buttons later, the car was moving and Allen replied: "what is it?"

"You remember that viral outbreak a couple of years ago? The one with the tainted blood?"

"Yeah," Williams said. "They called it SuperAIDS. Why?"

Reagan picked nervously at the hem of her suit skirt. "The Bureau had me investigate it."

"For what?"

"They wanted to know if it was some kind of intentional poisoning. I reviewed the patient files, talked to the Red Cross; I even met with the lead doctor working on the screening test for it."

"And?" asked Allen, taking his eyes off the road to steal a glance in Reagan's direction.

"Nothing. All of the doctors and the evidence said it was too complicated a scheme to be anything other than a short-lived spontaneous mutation."

"And now, because of this, you're second guessing that conclusion," Agent Williams said, reading his partner's mind.

"They're similar, right?"

"Meh. Yes and no," Allen answered. "They're both kind of medical in nature and people are dying, but that was a virus. The doctors in Pennsylvania told us this is bacteria. SuperAIDS was one person in each location and only after a blood transfusion. This is pockets of otherwise healthy people getting sick or dying." The car stopped at a red light and Allen turned to face his partner. "I get where you're coming from, but don't make this more complicated than it already is, okay?"

Reagan nodded. "Yeah, you're right." Just then noticing the line of gorgeous mansions stretching down the street they were on, she said: "where are we going?"

"Governor's Mansion. Special request from the Governor herself."

It was hard for Allen and Reagan to not be impressed by the stately Governor's Mansion in front of them as they slowly drove up the long path away from the gates and toward the office and home of Georgia's governor. The mansion itself was made of brick, with large white columns around each side and lush green grass surrounding the entire building. *Absolutely beautiful*, Reagan thought to herself.

Allen's words brought Reagan out of her reverie. "Ready?" he asked, putting their car in park in one of the reserved visitor's spots.

"Yep," Reagan replied with a nod. "Let's do this."

TWENTY-SEVEN

As they walked into the Georgia governor's well-appointed office, both Reagan and Allen were struck by the elegance and poise of the honorable Amy Murphy. But before the two FBI agents could fully process their surroundings and the impressive woman standing in front of them, an enormous Saint Bernard bounded over to them from behind the governor's desk and sat down directly in front of Allen, staring up at him.

Temporarily ignoring the massive dog, Governor Murphy offered a warm smile and stepped forward to shake hands with her visitors. "Welcome," the distinguished blonde said in a strong Southern accent, "I'm Amy Murphy. Y'all must be Agents Williams and White. And this," the governor added with a mock-scowl, "is our dog, Macy. She thinks this is her office."

Noticing that Allen appeared more than a little apprehensive with a 130-pound dog staring up at him, Mrs. Murphy quickly explained: "don't worry, she's harmless. Pet her for half a second and she'll leave you alone."

True to form, as soon as Allen gave the dog a quick pat on her oversized brown and white head, Macy stood up and ambled back over to plop down beside her owner's desk.

"Where are my manners?" Governor Murphy then asked with a self-deprecating smile. "Please, have a seat." Motioning to a brown leather couch pushed against one wall of the office, the governor herself sat down in a chair opposite the sofa. "Would y'all like anything to drink? Water? Tea?"

"No thank you," Agent Williams answered.

"No, we're fine. Thank you," Reagan agreed. The FBI agent tried hard not to stare, but the woman seated across from her was truly extraordinary. Nearly as tall as Reagan herself, Amy Murphy was athletic without looking too skinny like Reagan felt she always did, and the other woman hardly showed any of her forty-seven years. *Not to mention the fact that her suit probably cost more than I pay each month for rent*, Reagan thought. *And that's saying something in the DC market.*

"Okay," the governor said in response to the declined offer of drinks. When she then crossed one slender leg over the other, Reagan cut her eyes toward Allen, trying to see if he was checking out the attractive governor. Much to Agent White's surprise, her partner's eyes were focused straight back at her. An involuntary blush crept up Reagan's cheeks, and she was extremely grateful when Governor Murphy moved the conversation along.

"Let's get started," Murphy continued. "I know y'all have places to go and people to see, and I'm pretty busy myself." The governor paused to take a sip of sweet tea from the glass that an aide had silently brought into the room. "I asked y'all to come by this morning for a couple of reasons. First of all, I want to offer my assistance with your investigation. I hope it goes without saying, but I'll say it anyway: anything y'all need from me or my office, just let us know. The Georgia Bureau of Investigation and all of the affected sheriff's offices and police departments are also completely at your disposal."

"Thank you for that," Reagan replied. "We appreciate it."

Agent Williams nodded his head in agreement. "Yes ma'am, we sure do."

The governor responded with the half-smile for which she was famous, a grin that was big enough to bring out crinkles near her eyes but small enough that she didn't show her teeth. As Amy Murphy's political opponents quickly learned, the half-smile and its accompanying small dip of her chin was a highly effective tool. One couldn't help but like Mrs. Murphy when she did it.

"I'm glad to hear it," the poised politician continued, "and I'm glad to help." After another sip of tea, she added: "now about the other reason that I asked y'all to come. I want to coordinate our public messages. I know that the FBI's main spokesman and the White House Press Secretary have been handling things so far, but y'all are going to get pounded by the press here. Obviously," Murphy went on, gesturing with both of her hands as she spoke, "I don't want to step on the FBI's toes. But, at the same time, my office can't remain silent on the issue. Not when I've got nearly thirty citizens of my state either dead or in the hospital because of this thing that's now being called a biological weapon of mass destruction."

"Who called it that?" Allen interrupted.

"It was on the news this morning." Governor Murphy spread her fingers wide with her palms facing her guests to mimic the headline: "Possible WMD cause of flesh-eating bacteria deaths."

Allen sighed and looked down at the floor. "Shit."

As soon as the word came out of his mouth, Williams' eyes shot back up. "I'm so sorry. I didn't mean to say that out loud."

"Don't worry about it," the governor said, again with her engaging smile. "I've heard far worse."

No kidding, Reagan thought. During her flight from DC to Atlanta, Agent White researched Governor Murphy in order to prepare for their meeting. Reagan was amazed by what she discovered. Amy Murphy's maiden name was Millhouse, and when Amy Millhouse was twenty-two years old she was kidnapped by a violent drug gang in Mexico. What had been meant to be a celebratory college graduation trip with friends turned into a month-long nightmare. *After what she went through, I'm sure hearing a word like shit doesn't even faze her*. Reagan tried to prevent her face from displaying her thoughts, since the news articles she read also said that the governor didn't like to talk about her kidnapping.

With Allen embarrassed by his inadvertent cussing and Reagan lost in her thoughts about Amy Millhouse Murphy's past, the room fell silent. All anyone could hear was Macy the dog's panting in the corner.

"So?" Governor Murphy finally asked. "Do y'all have a preferred media strategy?"

Allen was the first to answer. "Yes ma'am. Yes, we do. We won't be taking any questions. As a rule, we do not comment on ongoing investigations. In your press conferences it would be appreciated if you could simply say that state and local officials are assisting with the investigation. And then you can also say anything you need or want to about steps to ensure clean water, any donation drives, or things like that."

Governor Murphy nodded her head in understanding. "Got it. Sounds good." The slender woman then uncrossed her legs and stood up from her chair, smoothing away non-existent wrinkles in her suit's skirt as she did. "I won't keep y'all any longer. I just wanted to make sure we were all on the same page. And to offer Georgia's help and support."

Allen and Reagan knew that was their cue. The two agents stood up almost in unison.

"Thank you for meeting with us, Governor," Reagan said. "I'm sure someone from Headquarters will keep your office up to date on the investigation."

"Excellent," the other woman replied as she shook hands with both of her guests.

At that exact moment, as if by magic, an aide to the governor opened her office door and stepped inside the room.

"Please make sure Agents Williams and White make it back to their car." Turning to her visitors, Murphy added: "this house is like a maze. I've been living here for five years and I still get lost sometimes."

"Right this way," the staffer said, motioning to his side and out the door.

Okay, Allen thought as he was led out of the Governor's Mansion, *political meeting is over. Now it's time to get to work.*

TWENTY-EIGHT

After leaving the ritzy Governor's Mansion, Reagan and Allen travelled to their significantly less spectacular hotel. The two agents checked into their rooms and decided to unpack before regrouping for lunch thirty minutes later.

While in his room, Agent Williams placed a call to FBI Headquarters in DC.

"Bruce Molina," his boss said as he answered the phone.

"Hey, sir, it's Allen Williams."

"Williams - any news out of Georgia?"

"Nothing so far, sir," Allen replied. "Agent White and I just finished meeting with Governor Murphy."

"What for?"

"Pledging her support, yada yada yada. But sir, listen, I have a favor to ask."

"What's that?" asked Molina.

"The Governor told us that news reports are talking about bioterrorism and weapons of mass destruction."

"So?"

"So can you tell the communications office to tone it down a little bit? People are already freaking out enough as it is. Repeatedly referencing WMDs and terrorism is just adding fuel to the fire."

Molina sighed into the phone. "Tell me this, Williams. Is there any doubt in your mind that we're dealing with a mass murderer?"

Allen didn't hesitate. "No sir."

"Any doubt at all that we're dealing with attacks on our water supply that are meant to inflict injury, illness, and public fear?"

"No sir."

"Then," the Assistant Deputy Director concluded, "it sounds like the Communications Office has it right."

"Yes sir, they do," Allen agreed. "I'm just saying that in a post-9/11 world, certain words scare people more than others. If they could just tone it down some. Rephrase things maybe."

His boss sighed again. "No guarantees, but I'll see what I can do."

****

About an hour after his phone call with ADD Molina, while sitting with Reagan at a diner near their hotel eating lunch, Allen's attention was drawn to the television set hanging on a wall. It was tuned to the local news station that was just starting its midday broadcast.

"We begin your news at noon with the ongoing story surrounding outbreaks of flesh-eating bacteria. For more on the latest developments, we'll go live to our correspondent, Bailey Greene, who is at one of the outbreak locations. Bailey?"

"Good afternoon, Matt. We are here live in Emerson, Georgia, a town about forty miles north of Atlanta that is the site of more bacterial outbreaks. After what was a relatively calm week as far as new cases are concerned, the bacteria came back with a vengeance yesterday. Eight people in Emerson are dead and another five have been hospitalized, bringing the total number of victims in our state to twenty-nine. An outbreak has also been reported in Farragut, Tennessee, which is a suburb of Knoxville.

"Now, Matt, I just got off the phone with an FBI spokesman in DC and he said this latest string of deaths and illnesses backs up the Bureau's early suspicions. The FBI is now all but confirming that these are man-made biological attacks, and that law enforcement agents across the country are now searching for a serial killer, a man they're referring to as the Flesh-Eating Bacteria, or F.E.B., Killer."

Taking another bite of his hamburger, Allen nodded with relief. *Bruce came through. People freak out a lot less when it's a serial killer instead of a terrorist.*

****

Reagan and Allen's next stop in Atlanta after lunch was the water treatment facility in the epicenter of the outbreak. The massive plant in the West Midtown neighborhood processed a significant portion of Atlanta's drinking water, and the two agents had scheduled a meeting with its Director of Operations.

A short, chubby man wearing baggy cargo pants and a 'Department of Public Works' golf shirt met Reagan and Allen at the plant's entrance. Introducing himself as A.J. Valencia, the Director of Operations suggested that they take a tour of the treatment facility and that he could answer any questions as they went along.

The first stop on the tour was the outdoor area comprised of large open-air water tanks. Reagan's eyes went immediately to the busy road running adjacent to the plant's fence.

"What kind of video surveillance do you have here?" she asked.

"Top of the line," Valencia replied. "I already told my security chief to start pulling the footage from the last several days and looking for anything suspicious." He pointed at various camera locations as he continued to walk. "We've got pretty much every area covered. Honestly the only place in the whole facility that isn't under video surveillance is the employee bathrooms."

Both of the FBI agents nodded their heads in approval. "We really would like to see those tapes," Allen added. "If you can get copies for us that'd be great. We'll want to send it up to our techs in DC."

"Sure thing man. Whatever you need."

Valencia then led the trio toward a group of buildings which housed all of the water cleaning machinery.

"When we spoke on the phone," Reagan said, "you told me there weren't any signs of a break-in recently. Is that still correct?"

"Yes ma'am. We double checked all of the fences and the locks. Nothing out of the ordinary."

This is just like Pennsylvania, Agent White thought. *No break-in to the treatment plant. But it can't be an inside job if they've hit two different sites now.*

"What about all of these fancy machines?" Allen asked. "Any signs of tampering? Changing the settings or anything like that so stuff gets through the filters that shouldn't? I read about that happening recently somewhere in Georgia."

The Director of Operations shook his head from side to side. "No sir, nothing like that. But I know what you're talking about. The facility that got hit was much smaller than and not nearly as high-tech as this place. It was up in some small town in the north Georgia mountains. The only security in place was a single chain-link fence. No cameras, no manned security presence." He shook his head again. "No way could you pull off something like that in my plant without someone knowing about it."

"Even if it was an inside job?"

Valencia bristled at the suggestion that any of his employees might go rogue, but he kept his composure and simply replied: "no way - even if it was an inside job. Too many cameras; too many security clearances to pass through in each building. A stunt like that would require entering at minimum three different buildings, and each building has its own entrance code. Not possible."

"Alright," Allen said. "We believe you. Now how about we go take a look at those surveillance tapes?"

****

Agents White and Williams spent the rest of their afternoon and evening scrolling through endless reels of security footage from the treatment plant. Four hours in, Allen reached his boredom limit.

"Come onnnnn, we already sent copies to the techs back at Headquarters. Can't we just let them review all of it? It's their job to do crap like this."

Reagan shook her head. "No, we can't. These tapes could be the big break we need. There wasn't any security footage in Pennsylvania . . . we need to take advantage of this resource while we have it."

Allen let out a disgruntled groan. "Fine. I'll keep watching."

"Good. I know it sucks, but this is what field work is like. Ninety percent boredom followed by ten percent craziness."

"No," Allen shook his head, "this isn't boredom. This is torture."

Reagan cut her eyes over at her partner. "Pay attention to your video. You might miss something."

Except he didn't miss anything. A solid seven hours spent watching video surveillance tapes from the water treatment plant and Reagan and Allen had nothing to show for it. No tampering with the purification settings; no cutting a hole in the razor-wire fence around the facility to sneak in. Just a whole bunch of nothing.

Which pretty much sums up the entire investigation so far, Reagan thought.

TWENTY-NINE

The next morning, Reagan knocked on Allen's hotel room door. She was already on her second cup of coffee and was ready to get started.

"It's unlocked!" her partner called out.

Agent White shook her head at Allen's slack security before opening the door and walking into his room. To her surprise, Williams was standing over a large map of the United States that was rolled out on his bed. Various articles of clothing were piled on the corners to keep the map from rolling up again.

Allen looked over at his partner as if he was the smartest man alive. "You know what this is?" he asked.

"A map?"

"Nope. *This*," Allen said, spreading his hands across the paper, "is how we're going to solve this case."

"With a map," Reagan repeated.

Allen huffed his disapproval. "You don't get it."

"Obviously not."

"He's leaving a trail," Allen explained. "All of the attacks are coming in lines. You can almost see him traveling between each spot."

"So we map where the outbreaks are and that will give us a general idea of our perp's home base."

"C'mon, this is a good idea," Williams said, grabbing a stack of post-it notes and a pen from the nightstand.

"Where did you get all of this stuff?" Reagan asked.

"CVS down the street. Like I said, I'm a morning person. Now get a pen and help me map this all out."

"I will," promised Reagan, "but there are a couple of problems with your plan, Einstein."

Allen stopped scribbling on the squares of paper and looked up. "Like what?"

"Well, to begin with," Reagan said, sitting down on the corner of the bed, "let's dispense with all of the 'he' talk. Every time anything really bad happens, everyone - from the public to the media to the authorities - assumes it's a guy. That cuts out half of our potential suspects without any justification for doing so."

Allen couldn't stop a smile from spreading across his face. A fact which irritated Reagan to no end.

"What could you possibly be smiling about?"

The smile tempered into a bemused grin. "You. It's a very bizarre form of feminism to say we have to make sure to remember that women can be evil too. But it's cute. It works for you."

Reagan sighed and rolled her eyes, standing up from the bed and folding her arms across her chest. "I'm going to pretend you didn't say that."

"What? The feminism part or the cute part?"

"Both."

Allen laughed. A deep, belly laugh that easily filled the small hotel room.

"Okay," he said. "That's one problem. What else is wrong with my map plan?"

Agent Williams noticed that his partner was relieved to have him shift the conversation back to work and away from his failed attempt at flirting. *Don't push it, dude*, Allen told himself. *You'll scare her away before you even get a real chance.*

Turning his attention back to the map and the task at hand, Allen managed to catch the tail end of Reagan's explanation that "even if we narrow it to one city, we're still potentially looking at millions of suspects. I mean, what if it's New York? That's over eight million people."

"Eight million is better than 350 million, or however big the United States population is now," Allen reasoned. "Look, answer me two things: will doing this out hurt our investigation?"

"No."

"Do you have any better ideas right now?"

Reagan sighed. "Unfortunately not."

"Then grab a pen and some post-it notes and start mapping."

THIRTY

A few hours later, for the second time in as many days, Reagan and Allen found themselves driving through Atlanta's upscale Buckhead neighborhood. This time, though, where they would've gone straight for the direction of the Governor's Mansion, Reagan turned their Bureau-issued black sedan down a side street and into the old money world of Tuxedo Park.

Reagan's jaw dropped at the sight of some of the gorgeous homes, and Allen did a fair bit of rubber-necking as well despite his own privileged upbringing.

Their destination was one of the less-palatial homes on the street, a sixties-era ranch belonging to the parents of bacteria victim Teddy Chandler. The two agents had barely exited their car when a gate in the backyard fence opened and a balding, middle-aged man with crying-induced bags under his eyes walked out. Trailing him was a rambunctious terrier that made a beeline for a group of rose bushes.

"Rambo! No!" the man yelled. "Get out of there! No!" The man reached the dog and picked him up right before he started digging. Carrying the terrier under one arm like a football, the homeowner then walked over toward the two black-suit clad visitors standing in the driveway.

"I'm sorry about that. Rambo here was my son's dog. I'm Peter Chandler. Y'all must be the FBI agents."

"We are," Reagan said. "I'm Agent White, and this is my partner Agent Williams. We'd like to ask you a few questions if that's alright."

"It's not alright," the grief-stricken father replied. "But you can. Come this way; my wife is out back in the sunroom."

Reagan and Allen followed the homeowner through the tall wooden fence and into a large, well-manicured backyard. Mr. Chandler closed the gate behind them and then put the appropriately-named Rambo down onto the grass. "Right this way," he said.

As she walked behind the two men, Reagan had a flash vision of the last time she went around investigating mysterious deaths. *The Hernandez's house in New York. The handsome Hispanic man who lost his wife and baby.* She sighed. *And before that there was Mrs. Russell in Baltimore.* Another heavy sigh escaped Reagan's lips. *This is the worst part of the job.*

Peter Chandler opened the door into the sunroom, a brightly-lit space with plush patio furniture and wall-to-wall windows. Seated on one of the couches was a woman who looked to be around the same age as her husband. Next to Mrs. Chandler, with his head resting on her lap, was a giant Goldendoodle. The miniature lion lifted his head briefly to assess the visitors, decided they weren't a threat, and plopped it back down again.

"This is my wife, Pam," Mr. Chandler said. "And this is our dog, Max. He's too damn smart for his own good . . . he knows something is wrong and hasn't left Pam's side since we got the news about Teddy and Asher."

Mrs. Chandler nodded. "Sweet puppy," she said, patting the one hundred pound 'puppy' on the head.

"Nice to meet you," Allen said. "Like we told your husband, I'm Agent Williams and this is Agent White. We'd like to ask you a few questions about your son and your nephew."

Mr. Chandler joined his wife on the couch, on the opposite side of the dog. "We'll give you whatever answers you need. We - " He paused, trying to hold back tears. "We just want to find out what happened."

"So do we," Reagan replied. She reached down into her briefcase and pulled out a notepad and pen, the déjà vu hitting again. "First of all, before we get started, I want to say how very sorry we are for your loss."

"Thank you," Mrs. Chandler said, tears beginning to fill her eyes.

"We'll try to keep this as short as possible. Your son lived in West Midtown, across the street from a large water treatment facility. Is that correct?"

"Yes."

"And Mr. Randall, your nephew, was just visiting?"

Peter Chandler nodded. "Yeah. He's my sister's son. Asher lives - or, lived - in London. He was on vacation."

"And when is the last time you saw either of them?" Allen asked.

"I hadn't seen Asher since last summer. I saw Teddy a couple weeks ago, and all three of us were supposed to play golf that morning."

"Teddy and I had lunch together last Wednesday," his mom chimed in. "That's the last time I saw him. He was so excited about Asher coming in town."

"Did everything seem normal when you met with them? Anything out of the ordinary?" Allen pressed.

Both parents shook their heads. "No, everything seemed fine," the mother replied.

Reagan wrote down their answers and nodded. "I know this might be difficult, but did either man have any enemies that you know of? Anyone who might want to hurt them?"

"No, nobody."

"We obtained copies of your nephew's police file in England," Allen said. "He was arrested four times during high school and college for trespass. Your son also had a juvenile record for trespass and destruction of property."

Mrs. Chandler sat up defensively. "They were childish pranks."

"Those records were supposed to be sealed," her husband added.

Allen, less experienced in the field than Reagan, adopted a more combative tone. "The water poisonings are being examined as potential acts of terrorism. The PATRIOT Act gives us broad investigative powers."

Reagan knew she needed to play good cop and diffuse the situation. "We are not at all considering either your son or your nephew as suspects. What my partner was trying to say was that, given their prior incidents, do you think it's possible that they had a bit too much to drink the night before and decided to sneak into the treatment plant? One more prank, just like old times?"

"No." Mrs. Chandler stared daggers at both of the visitors and, sensing his owner's stress, Max issued a warning growl.

"I think it's about time for you two to leave," Peter Chandler said. "You know the way out."

Reagan nodded and stood up from her wicker chair, with Allen following suit. "Of course. Thank you both for your time. If you think of anything else that might be helpful to the investigation, here's my card. Please don't hesitate to call."

The investigators left the sunroom and crossed through the backyard, careful to close the fence gate behind them.

"Well that was a total bust," Allen said as they got back into their car.

"It's generally not a good idea to suggest to a victim's relatives that their loved ones were terrorists," Reagan scolded her partner.

"I never said that."

"Yeah, you kind of did," she responded. "Look, you're very good at what you do. But this, interviewing people and looking for leads, this is what I do. So how about we let me take point on future interviews?"

"Fine," Allen replied. "Whatever. But I did not call them terrorists."

"Allen?"

"What?"

"Are you going to start the car?"

Agent Williams realized that they were still sitting in the Chandler's driveway. "Oops. Yeah." He cranked the engine. "Where to next, oh great investigator?"

"Lunch," Reagan said. "I'm starving."

THIRTY-ONE

Huddled back at their hotel for a working lunch, Agents White and Williams spread out their interview notes and a variety of food on the spare bed in Reagan's room.

"Go with me for a minute on this," Allen began in between mouthfuls of takeout food.

"Okay," Reagan replied. She was used to her partner's thought process by now. He came up with usually outlandish theories, and it was her job to try to glean the useful parts from whatever he said.

"We know the bacteria is being transmitted through the water, right? The drinking water to be exact. And at first everyone started running out to by those Brita water filters, thinking that would keep them safe."

"But the tests were inconclusive," Reagan recalled. "The filters can help some but wouldn't be able to stop a large amount of bacteria."

"Right. So now what's the big thing everyone is doing? Buying bottled water. Stores can't keep it in stock."

Reagan finished chewing her food, swallowed, then asked: "what's your point?"

"What if the bottled water companies are behind it? Evian and Dasani and whoever else banding together and sabotaging the water supply. Think about it: people aren't going to trust tap water for years."

Agent White sighed and pursed her lips together, thinking about Allen's most recent theory. "It seems a bit much, don't you think?"

"The whole thing seems a bit much to me," Agent Williams answered. "We've spent billions of dollars to develop accurate mechanisms for testing and cleaning our drinking water, and now you'd probably be safer drinking the water in a Third World country than you are in the United States."

"Not exactly," Reagan corrected.

"Oh, you know what I mean. But admit it: the water company theory *is* possible. Not probable, I admit. But possible."

****

Back in Bethesda at the National Institutes of Health, Joseph was in a great mood. News reports about his bacteria grew increasingly worried and frantic with every passing day, and the changes he made between the first and second weekend of attacks ensured that victims were dying quickly and in high numbers.

This is going really well, he thought with a smile.

As was common in their third-story offices, Keri Dupree walked into Joseph's workspace unannounced. The doctor opened her mouth to say something and then paused, warily eyeing the glass of water sitting on her boss' desk.

"Is that bottled?" Keri asked.

Dr. Carlson lifted his head up from the stack of papers he had been reading. "Is what bottled?"

"That water," she answered, pointing at the glass.

"Oh. No. Why?"

"Have you been living under a rock? A water-borne bacteria is popping up all over the country. Don't even try to say you don't know about it . . . I get the same email alerts that you do from the CDC."

The man Keri knew as Isaac shrugged his shoulders and sighed. "Yeah, I know what you're talking about. But none of the outbreaks have been around here, so I don't see a need to avoid perfectly safe drinking water."

"I'm sure that's what they said in Atlanta three days ago," Keri replied. "Come to think of it," she continued, "why aren't we working that case? We did the last big illness outbreak."

"The blood virus was different," Dr. Carlson answered. "Nobody knew what was killing people. They know what this is. They just can't stop it."

Keri wasn't satisfied with that answer. "So why aren't we working on a way to stop it?"

Isaac sighed again, took off his glasses, and rubbed his fingers over his tired eyes. Looking back up at his assistant, he said: "I liked you a lot better before you had mommy hormones racing through your body. You get too emotional about everything now."

Dr. Dupree pursed her lips together angrily but didn't reply, so Isaac continued. "This water thing is a bacteria. How do you stop those? Antibiotics. Come on - this is elementary stuff. The particular bacteria infecting people right now is resistant to our current crop of drugs, and it could take years to come up with another line of better, stronger antibiotics. Plus there are already a ton of labs and companies working on that."

Carlson could tell that Keri still wasn't satisfied enough to drop the issue and go back to work. So he added one more lie for good measure. "Look, I understand that you're worried. A flesh-eating bacteria is a scary thing. An antibiotic-resistant flesh-eating bacteria is a very scary thing. And I understand your desire to use your medical expertise to solve the problem. I have that same desire. But I called the CDC and my superiors in the Department of Health and Human Services and they told me that the best bet for stopping this thing is to go after whoever is poisoning the water. It's a matter for the FBI, not the doctors."

Dr. Dupree issued an exasperated sigh and rolled her eyes. "Why didn't you just tell me that in the first place?"

"What, that I called people?"

"And offered our help but they said no. Yeah. That's all you had to say."

"Okay then," Isaac replied, holding up his hands in mock surrender. "I offered our help and they said no. Now that that's settled, can I get back to work?"

"No, actually. I have something for you." The Deputy Chief of Pathology then held out a white card with sparkles and lace attached to it. "It's an invitation to my son's Christening."

"I'm certainly no expert on church stuff, but isn't he a little old for that?" Dr. Carlson asked.

Keri shrugged. "Yeah. We weren't going to do it at all, but Scott's parents have been bugging us about it ever since Matty was born. We're not super religious but they are, so we kind of figured what could it hurt, right?"

Dr. Carlson stared back at his assistant. "That's the dumbest thing I've ever heard."

"Well, then, don't come. I didn't figure you would anyway. But now you can't say you weren't invited."

"Keri?" Isaac said.

"Yeah?"

"Leave. I have work to do."

"Ugh, fine. Whatever," she said in a huff. Pointing again at his glass of water, Keri added: "I'm buying you a case of bottled water, though. And you're going to drink it. Whether you want to or not."

****

Hours after his conversation with Dr. Dupree, Joseph was still amused by her concern over his drinking water. *Like I would actually drink something that I thought could be poisoned.* Carlson shook his head. *I'm the only person in the country who knows which water is safe and which isn't.* The doctor smiled and sank down into the leather couch in his living room. "Time to watch the latest episode of my favorite reality show: United States Under Attack."

As Joseph quickly observed, American television's talking heads had followed the same routine every night since government officials announced they thought the water was being intentionally poisoned. Broadcasts began with an update on any new outbreaks, and then gave reports about the condition of those already infected. Next they issued some statement to the effect of "we still don't have a clue who is behind the attacks," followed by a commercial break.

The latter half of the nightly segment was always devoted to some version of the same conversation: *is this what life in America is like now?* Counterterrorism experts and immigrants from places like Israel or Northern Ireland would wax poetic about how the United States was simply experiencing what life in other countries was like, speaking unwelcome truths about living under constant, palpable threat of terror attacks. The newscasters would mention events such as 9/11, the DC snipers, and the Boston Marathon bombings, and people watching at home would temporarily look up from their smart phones and other e-gadgets, nod their heads, and have flash memories of where they were when those other terror attacks happened.

It would then be the patriotic reporters' turn to jump in again, categorically denying the fact that America could ever turn into anything like the Gaza Strip or other war-torn areas. "Our police forces and intelligence officers are too good," they would argue. "The government thwarts the vast majority of planned attacks before they even come close to happening," another might say. Not to be outdone by: "the American public is much more vigilant than it used to be."

A statement to which one prosecutor-turned-defense attorney would reply: "you can't stop the lone wolf."

And the talking heads would bobble up and down in agreement, knowing they were really only passing time while waiting for yet another person to be announced dead due to complications from the water-borne flesh eating bacteria.

THIRTY-TWO

By the time Joseph Carlson began packing for his next weekend trip, twenty-two people were dead. Five in Pennsylvania and seventeen more in Georgia and Tennessee. Another twenty-eight were still hospitalized with symptoms related to Joseph's bacteria. Things were looking up.

It took Dr. Carlson nine and a half hours to drive from his home in North Bethesda to the site of his next drop: Greenfield, Indiana. Joseph didn't have any patient appointments or meetings that Friday, so he told Dr. Dupree and the overeager office receptionist, Lois, that he would be working in his home lab that day. After work and a quick dinner at home on Thursday night, Dr. Carlson loaded up his car and hit the road.

"This place better be good," Joseph said to his empty car when he spotted an interstate sign that read 'Greenfield: forty miles.' Below Greenfield on the sign was Indianapolis, another thirty miles down the road. "I'm damn tired and certainly don't need any complications," Joseph continued. "Especially not any more Children of the Corn scenes like that place in Georgia." He shook his head. "Nowhere should ever be that quiet."

Quiet wouldn't be a problem now for the doctor, since early morning commuters were already hitting the roads on their way into Indianapolis. Joseph turned the volume down on his satellite radio and started to pay more attention to the map in the passenger seat beside him. "I should be making a right sometime soon."

Five more turns and ten minutes later, Dr. Carlson saw his mark in the distance. "Hello, Greenfield Reservoir and Water Treatment Facility," he said with a smile. "Nice to see you."

Joseph pulled his car into the still empty parking lot of an office complex. Thirty minutes later and there would've been witnesses. But not now; not at five-thirty in the morning when the only people awake were still in a pre-coffee haze.

Knowing he needed to work quickly, Carlson opened his trunk and began loading the bacteria-soaked paper from its cooler into the potato gun. Glancing over his shoulder, he was relieved to see that the parking lot remained empty.

The doctor then shut the hatch of the trunk, climbed back into the driver's seat, and pulled onto the two-lane highway that conveniently passed right by the water treatment plant.

Joseph rolled down the window of his car and took a firmer grip on the potato gun. He had the drop process down to a science now.

Checking his rearview mirror to make sure there were no cars behind him, he slowed down below the already slow thirty-five mile per hour speed limit. A food delivery truck sped by going in the opposite direction. Joseph took a deep breath, lifted the launcher up and out the window, and fired.

Three deadly paper balls flew across the street and over the barbed wire fence with ease, splashing down unnoticed into Greenfield's supply of drinking water. The sleepy Midwestern bedroom community had just been attacked by a biological weapon of mass destruction, and its residents had no idea.

****

When his supply of Red Bull and copious amounts of sugar candy weren't cutting it anymore, Joseph knew he needed to sleep. He pulled off Interstate 70 near Richmond, Indiana, about an hour east of Greenfield and two and a half hours west of his next stop in Zanesville, Ohio. Finding an old strip mall that had seen better days, Joseph brought his car to a stop and parked in an empty space next to a lamppost. There were two tractor-trailer cabs parked at the other end of the complex, but aside from that Dr. Carlson was alone. "Well, it's no Ritz Carlton, but it'll do." He then locked the doors, placed his gun on his lap just in case, and closed his eyes.

The cell phone alarm Joseph had set started going off two hours later, the noise so startling that the doctor almost shot himself in the leg by accident.

"Holy shit," he said, putting the safety back on the gun and storing it away in the car's console. "No more sleeping with guns."

Joseph shook his head back and forth to make sure he was fully awake. He checked his watch. Eight-thirty. *Man, I have to pee.*

Spotting a fast food restaurant across the street, Joseph cranked his car. Just as quickly, he turned it off. "Drop prep. C'mon, Joe. Get your head in the game."

The doctor then exited his car and walked around to the trunk to get his next round of bacteria ready for launch. Two-to-three hours was the perfect amount of time to soak the paper in the petri dishes: long enough for the bacteria to fully work its way into the material, but not so long that the paper started to break apart.

His prep work complete, Joseph got back into his car and drove in the direction of dirty bathrooms and greasy heart attacks on buns. After that, it was next stop: Zanesville.

****

Dr. Carlson liked what little he saw of Zanesville, Ohio. It had a cute downtown area that looked to be in the process of restoration, and even a cynic like Joseph had to admit that it was cool to drive on the city's famous Y-Bridge and make a left-hand turn right there in the middle of the river.

But the doctor's sightseeing expedition didn't last long. Zanesville's water treatment facility was a sprawling complex just south of town and right next to the river. Joseph knew he had to be careful making a drop in the middle of the day, but it actually helped that it was a Friday and not the weekend. Directly adjacent to the plant was a city park and dozens of playing fields.

Come tomorrow that place will be crawling with snot-nosed kids and helicopter parents, Joseph thought. *Also known as witnesses. But not today.*

The potato gun shot went off without a hitch, up and over yet another razor wire fence and with an undetected splashdown.

Joseph allowed himself the luxury of a small smile. Everything was going according to plan.

THIRTY-THREE

As Dr. Carlson made his way east along Interstate 70, a stay-at-home mom in Greenfield, Indiana named Sasha Gomez was winding down her morning routine.

Sasha liked routines. She had a schedule for everything. A list for everything. A plan for everything. And as her husband and kids knew, God help the person who messed up her routine.

On this particular Friday morning, the next to last of the school year, the thirty-two year old Mrs. Gomez did what she always did on Fridays when class was in session. Her husband, Tim, was out of town on a business trip and wouldn't return home until later that night, so Sasha only had to worry about getting her two kids on the bus to their local elementary school. Evan and Mackenzie, eight and six respectively, woke up promptly at 6:15am. Breakfast on Fridays was always toast (whole wheat, of course) and freshly cut fruit. Then it was time to get the two dressed and out the door to the neighborhood street corner by 7:03 on the dot. Her kids' bus driver was always on time, something that Sasha appreciated. She liked routines.

The stay-at-home mom caught a glimpse of her favorite morning show on TV while she cleaned up the kitchen and had her own breakfast of organic yogurt. Aside from her routines, Mrs. Gomez was known for one other thing: she was a health nut. *Not like that's a bad thing*, Sasha thought as she dropped her spoon into the sink and tossed the empty yogurt container in the recycling bin. *No preservatives, no caffeine, and as much farm-fresh food as possible. The way humans were meant to eat.*

Sasha reached for the remote and turned up the volume when the talk show hosts began discussing the flesh-eating bacteria that had already killed several people in the United States.

"I don't understand how this is even possible," one of the women said, her brunette hair bouncing up and down as she gestured wildly around her.

Me neither, thought Sasha.

"I mean, we clean our water," the TV personality continued. "This isn't just some hipsters out on a nature walk who are getting sick. This is city tap water. *Purified* city tap water. I don't get it."

"Well," her co-host replied, "we are lucky in that we have with us here today an expert in infectious diseases who is going to explain to our viewers what is going on. Everyone, let's give a warm welcome to Dr. Gill Pingrey from the Centers for Disease Control."

The audience clapped and Sasha Gomez sat riveted to her chair, wanting to hear the doctor's explanation.

"Dr. Pingrey," the co-host continued, "like my colleague just said, how is this water poisoning even possible?"

The attractive young doctor with floppy brown hair and ice blue eyes didn't have to work hard to have a captive audience.

"Well," he said with a thick Southern drawl, "first of all, thank you for having me on your show. My wife watches y'all all the time." He paused. "Regarding the poisoned water, let me first say that flesh-eating bacteria is very rare but very serious. The medical term for it is necrotizing fasciitis, and about one in four people who get NF will die from it."

The show's host interrupted. "I thought the FBI said that this wasn't actually necrotizing fasciitis."

Dr. Pingrey nodded. "That's correct. Patients have been testing negative for that specific bacteria. Nonetheless, all of their symptoms are the same. What we believe has happened is that the bacteria mutated. That's actually fairly common . . . one type of bacteria will alter itself a little bit. What is making this particular bacteria so difficult to treat is that it's resistant to our antibiotics."

"It's a superbug," the co-host said.

"Yes," Dr. Pingrey agreed. "The bacteria that is being used by the so-called FEB Killer is what we refer to as a carbapenem-resistant enterobacteriaceae. A CRE, for short."

"Well, that's a mouthful!" the TV personality replied. "But back to my original question, how is there any bacteria in our drinking water? We have massive water treatment plants all over the place. I drive past them all the time."

Dr. Pingrey grimaced. "That's the million dollar question. The purification facilities that you're talking about have multi-step, highly sophisticated processes for cleaning the water that we drink. I won't bore y'all with the details, but basically the water goes through filters and sifters and many rounds of chemical treatments before it ever reaches your tap. And," he sighed, "to be honest with you, we don't know how the FEB Killer is doing it. The FBI is working around the clock trying to figure it out, and my team at the CDC is assisting in every way we can. All we can really say right now is to make sure you filter or boil your water, and buy bottled water if possible."

****

Despite being a few minutes late for exercising after watching the television interview with the CDC guy, Mrs. Gomez was still in a good mood that morning as she went back upstairs to change into her running clothes. A combination of the near end of the school year, her husband getting back that night, and a block party on their street the next day had the suburban woman excited. *It's going to be a good weekend*, she thought with a smile.

Part of being a health nut meant that Sasha Gomez also exercised six days a week. The weather was sunny and not yet too hot, so she decided to run outside that day. The former high school track star was almost out the door when she stopped and turned around. "Almost forgot my water bottle," she said to the family cat, Socks, who was perched on a chair watching her owner. "That wouldn't be good - I'm doing eight miles today." Sasha quickly returned to the kitchen and filled up her plastic bottle with water from her Brita filter. Like most moms she knew, Sasha was being extra careful to only drink filtered water.

"Okay, all set," she said, screwing the cap back on the bottle. "See ya in a little while, Socks."

The slender Mrs. Gomez was three and a half miles into her run through Greenfield's quiet suburban streets, almost to her turnaround spot, when she started to feel sick. Sasha slowed her pace from a run to a jog, and then further to a walk, as the rumblings in her stomach grew stronger and the nausea crept up in her throat. "Holy crap. What was in that yogurt?"

The runner's hands clutched her stomach in pain, and seconds later the pale strawberry color of her breakfast splattered onto the shoulder of the road. Sasha stumbled sideways, continuing to vomit but nevertheless trying to make sure she was out of the way in case any cars drove by. The woman could feel her hands turn clammy. Her vision blurred. *What in the world is happening?*

Sasha's liquid projectiling was growing redder and redder in color with each passing round, the strawberry yogurt being replaced by blood. The world then also started to spin, and the woman who thirty minutes earlier had been the picture of health collapsed onto the ground, her body in shock as it rolled down the adjacent ditch and out of sight of any potential passersby.

****

Amanda Leibowitz lived next door to the Gomez's and, although they didn't socialize much, Amanda thought Sasha was a good mom and a nice enough neighbor. Consequently, Mrs. Leibowitz was surprised that when her kids walked in the door from school that afternoon, the two Gomez children followed.

"Umm, hi Evan. Hi Mackenzie. What are you two doing here? Where's your mom?"

The third-grader, Evan, shrugged his shoulders. "I dunno. She wasn't at the bus stop when we got there, and she said if that ever happened to go to a neighbor's house."

Although the little boy didn't seem concerned, and since his sister took her cues from her older brother she didn't look worried either, something didn't feel right to Mrs. Leibowitz. It wasn't like Sasha Gomez to not be there when her kids got home from school. There had been a few times in the past when Sasha missed the bus because she got stuck in traffic while running errands, but even then she had called Amanda and asked her if she could watch the kids until their mom got back.

Trying to stay calm and not upset the four children in the room with her, Amanda took a deep breath and walked over to the kitchen counter where her phone was. "Okay," she said. "Let's just call your mom's cell phone and find out where she is."

The line rang five times before clicking over to voicemail.

"Hmm, that's weird," said Mrs. Leibowitz. Shoving her cell phone into the back pocket of her jeans, Amanda opened a kitchen drawer and pulled out a spare key that was marked 'Gomez.' Sasha and Tim had given their neighbors the key in case they ever needed to get into the house for any reason. *Now would be one of those reasons*, Amanda thought.

"Alright," she said to the kids, "you four stay here. I'm going to run next door and make sure your mom didn't just fall asleep in the bathtub or anything like that."

"Mommy doesn't take baths," little Mackenzie corrected. "She says they're too dirty because you just sit in the yucky water."

Amanda smiled at the six year old. "Okay, well I'm going to go over there and check anyway. Don't leave the house while I'm gone."

Just as their neighbor suspected, the Gomez house was empty. "Where is she?" Amanda asked aloud.

A cat hopped off the kitchen table and made Amanda jump. Something else on the table caught her eye: Sasha's cell phone. Picking it up off the counter, Mrs. Leibowitz saw that her neighbor had twenty-six unread emails, seven unread texts, three Facebook notifications, and five missed calls.

"This isn't right," Amanda said. "Something isn't right. The only time Sasha doesn't have her phone is when she goes running. But that would've been hours ago."

Amanda checked the missed calls. One was from her a few minutes earlier, but the other four were from Sasha's husband. He was looking for her too.

****

The search for Sasha Gomez took longer than people initially thought it would. Her husband Tim caught an early flight and arrived home at 5pm, an hour and half into Amanda Leibowitz's search. The neighbor had already called the police, only to be informed that she had to wait until Mrs. Gomez was missing for twenty-four hours before filing a report. Amanda had also loaded the kids into her SUV and driven around the neighborhood streets where Sasha was known to run. No luck.

Thirty-five year old Tim Gomez had long ago shed his coat and tie. His shirt sleeves were rolled up to the elbows and his hair was standing on end after being pulled at its roots so many times in the past few hours.

Standing in his kitchen with several of his neighbors, Tim decided it was time to take action.

"Amanda, can you take the kids to your house? Everybody else: I'm going to walk Sasha's running route. I could use all of the extra eyes and ears I can get."

Amanda nodded in agreement and went to gather up Evan and Mackenzie to take to her house. *I have no idea how I can distract them, but it's at least worth a shot*, she thought.

The rest of the crowd dispersed back to their homes to gather flashlights and other search materials. A group of twenty joined back up in the Gomez's driveway a few minutes later.

"Okay everybody. We're going to fan out along the route that Sasha likes to run. Don't break the line; walk slowly. I don't want to overlook anything."

The search party found Sasha an hour and a half later. Face down in a roadside ditch, covered in dried mud, sweat, and vomit.

Nineteen concerned friends and neighbors gathered on the shoulder of the road and looked down into the ditch, watching as Tim sat in the dirt and held his wife in his arms, rocking her gently as if she was sleeping.

The FEB Killer had come to Indiana.

THIRTY-FOUR

A few hours earlier and farther east in Zanesville, completely unaware of the events unfolding in Greenfield, Courtney Douglass was sitting down to lunch with two of her friends. The three middle-aged women had met to eat and socialize at a trendy restaurant in Zanesville's revitalized downtown district.

One thing Courtney's friends had learned about her was that she didn't do permanent. Two marriages but neither stuck. A coke habit in the '80s that she kicked with relative ease. Family - and friends - who came and went. Even Courtney's photographs, the ones by which she earned her modest income, were almost always of people or objects in motion. No, Courtney Douglass didn't do permanent. Until she moved to Zanesville, Ohio that is.

"Do y'all know this is the longest I've ever lived in the same place?" Courtney asked the two other women, the 'y'all' a lasting reminder of her childhood in various towns in south Alabama. "Yep, I've been here for four years now. I can't believe it."

The fifty-two year old woman with shoulder-length dyed brown hair leaned back into her chair and smiled. "Four years, and for the first time in my life I'm not itching to move again."

"That's great, Court," said her friend and fellow artist Diana McGee. She and a local sculptor, Christina Langdon, had met Courtney at a street festival a few years earlier and the three women became instant friends.

"It really is," Christina added. "You know what else is great? This weather!"

All three women smiled in agreement, turning their heads up to face the sun. Winter had been particularly long and harsh that year in their central Ohio town, and the restaurant's outdoor, riverfront patio was packed with people like Courtney and her friends, all seeking to take advantage of Friday's gorgeous weather.

"I think this - the weather and Court's four years here - deserve to be celebrated," Diana said. "It's noon, right? Where's the waiter . . . let's get some wine."

"Oh, just water for me," Courtney corrected. "Y'all know I can't hold my alcohol and I have to drive out to Dillon Lake for a shoot this afternoon."

As if on cue, a waiter appeared to take the ladies' order. "Two glasses of chardonnay and one glass of water, please," said Christina. "Filtered water," she added.

"Of course," the waiter nodded. "That's all we serve now." The college-age young man disappeared to get the drinks.

"Not to put a damper on things," Diana said, "but have you all been paying attention to that flesh-eating bacteria thing? With the poisoned water?"

"You might want to change what you're drinking," Christina half-joked to her friend. "You probably have less of a chance of getting hurt drinking and driving than you do having water right now."

Courtney sighed and rolled her eyes. "I do not. Don't be ridiculous. Besides, all of the outbreaks have been way east of here, and we get our drinking water straight from that river," she said, pointing to the body of water slowly flowing past them and through the city.

The waiter reappeared. "Here you go, ladies. Two chardonnays and a water." After handing out the drinks, he said, "have you decided what you want to eat?"

Diana glanced at her friends, who both nodded. "Yep, we're ready," she answered. "I'd like the turkey club, no mayonnaise."

"Chicken caesar salad for me," Courtney said.

"And I would like the risotto, please," added Christina.

After the waiter left, Courtney took a long, exaggerated sip of water from her glass. "See? Nothing to worry about."

As soon as the words left her mouth, the women heard a commotion inside the restaurant. "Call 911!" someone yelled.

Diana called over to a couple who were seated by the restaurant's glass window. "What's going on?"

"Hard to tell," the man answered. "There's a big crowd of people around one table, but it looks like there's a man lying on the floor."

About to say 'that's horrible,' Courtney felt a deep rumbling in her stomach, followed by a sudden wave of nausea. "I'm gonna - " she paused, swallowing back the oncoming sickness. Courtney stood up from the table. "I'm not . . . I'm not feeling well. I'm going to go to the restroom."

Her friends looked up with worry. "You okay?" Christina asked.

Courtney nodded, albeit unconvincingly. She turned to make her way toward the door inside, each step harder than the one prior. *My legs hurt*, she thought. *Hell, all of me hurts.*

The woman stopped, put her hand up to cover her mouth, and then took it away just as quickly. Courtney spewed the contents of her stomach all over the floor, table, and people in front of her.

"I'm sorry, I'm so . . . uuuunghhhhh." A second round of vomit poured out.

Courtney tried to move, tried to keep walking and somehow find the bathroom or at least a trash can, but her feet felt like they were tied to cinder blocks. All she could do was stand there, continuing to throw up all over the now unoccupied table.

Christina rushed to her friend's side to help, even if all that entailed was holding back her hair.

Something resembling woman's intuition hit Diana. *The water. Oh my God, the water.* She pulled out her cell phone and dialed 911. "Hello? Yes, I need an ambulance at

Augustine's on the riverfront. My friend is really sick. I think she's been poisoned."

The emergency operated sounded irritated. "As I've already told numerous callers, there is an ambulance on its way right now."

"No no no. You don't understand. They called about the guy inside. We need another ambulance for my friend. I'm not kidding, this is not a prank: I think Zanesville's water has been poisoned."

THIRTY-FIVE

Hours after Joseph's latest round of victims fell ill, the medical researcher arrived at his third drop location: Morgantown, West Virginia. It reminded Joseph of Emerson, Georgia, and he didn't like that. Not so much the size . . . Emerson was a small town while Morgantown housed a major university. Rather, the similarity was in the quiet. Joseph had planned on Morgantown, West Virginia being a daytime drop as well, but his lack of sleep had caught up to him yet again on the drive from Ohio to West Virginia. An impromptu six hour 'nap' meant it was now after dark in the land of the Mountaineers. Even though it was a Friday, on the outskirts of the city and away from West Virginia University everything was quiet. On that stretch of highway, where the crickets threatened to drown out his radio, Joseph finally found the water treatment plant.

"Shit," the budding terrorist said, the word dragging out as he drove past the entrance to the facility. Unlike most of his other drops, and reminiscent again of Emerson, this treatment plant was located at the end of short strip of roadway adjacent to the highway. *No drive-by shooting here*, Joseph thought.

He pulled a U-turn at the next red light and circled back around to his drop site. *Just get it over with before the inbred sheriff catches you out here.* West Virginia, as far as Joseph was concerned, was no more than a trash dump teeming with other states' rejects. A night in jail in these parts was the last thing the Ivy League elitist wanted.

The access road to the water treatment facility was wide and newly-paved. *Undoubtedly the result of pork barrel spending in Congress*, Joseph thought. Grabbing a baseball hat and sunglasses out of the back seat, Joseph put them on and quickly exited his car. He walked up to the edge of the tall, razor-wire fence that blocked his entry. Lifting the spud gun to his shoulder, the doctor took aim and fired.

Three highly sophisticated spit balls flew up and over the fence, easily clearing the razor wire. Too easily, in fact. All three disease delivery devices fell victim to gravity, landing on a concrete sidewalk with a splat.

"Shit!"

Joseph sprinted back to his car and opened the trunk. *Thank God I had already started to prep the Harrisonburg drop.* The doctor quickly loaded another round of his biological weapon into the CO_2-powered launcher and went back to the fence, this time careful to stand farther away to have a better angle.

The second launch was successful, and from liftoff to splashdown lasted maybe four seconds.

Joseph breathed a sigh of relief. The paper balls he just shot were all he had left in the cooler. If those had failed, he would've been behind on two drop locations instead of just one. One alone was already unacceptable.

Dr. Carlson returned to his car and backed down the plant's access road toward the highway.

"Alright, people of Harrisonburg, Virginia," he said, "you've been granted a stay of execution. For now."

THIRTY-SIX

Saturday morning in Washington, DC brought news of more bacterial outbreaks. The FEB Killer had struck again, and everyone from President Hughes to Agent White and back again was pulling their hair out trying to solve the case.

Daniel Bader was one of those people, the Chief of Staff's thinning gray hair seemingly falling out in clumps due to stress.

"Dannyyyyyyyyy!"

Bader sighed and stood up from his desk. "On my way, Mr. President," he called out, putting on his suit jacket and walking toward the door that connected his workspace with the Oval Office. The sigh came from knowing what President Hughes wanted: for the past two weeks, ever since news broke of the first bacterial outbreak, 'Danny' had become synonymous with 'why the hell haven't we solved this yet?'

"Yes sir?" the Chief of Staff asked as he entered the new room.

Hughes held up a newspaper in his hand. "Did you see today's *Post*? 'FEB Killer Strikes Again.' Or how about this one in the *Times*: 'Hughes Helpless as Outbreak Spreads West.' Why the hell haven't we solved this yet?"

"We're using every resource we have, Mr. President. The FBI, Joint Terrorism Task Force, and state and local law enforcement are working around the clock. The public is also being much more careful. Anyone who can is avoiding tap water and drinking bottled."

The president snorted his disapproval. "Yeah, and now I've got the minority caucuses riding my ass saying the bacteria is racist because poor people can't afford to buy bottled water."

"Yes sir, I know. And we're coordinating with agencies and charities to try to get water to people who need it. But we can't bottle water for three hundred million people."

President Hughes let out a deep breath. "I know. I'm sorry, Bader, it's not your fault. The headlines just struck a nerve. I do feel helpless - just sitting around waiting for the next attack."

"I know. We all feel that way, sir." The Chief of Staff paused, an idea coming to him. "There is something we can do to improve your image regarding the attacks."

"What?"

"Publicize a meeting, here, with the Homeland Security Secretary and the FBI Director. Maybe bring in the two agents in charge of the investigation."

Hughes thought about it for a second. "Yes, yes, yes, and no. The agents are busy enough. I don't want them taking focus off the investigation to come talk to me."

"Okay," the Chief of Staff nodded. "I'll start putting the rest of it together."

****

Agent Williams arrived at FBI Headquarters at eight o'clock on Saturday morning to find Reagan already working. The pair had returned from Atlanta a few days earlier and now spent the majority of their time in a conference room near Reagan's cramped office.

"Your cat is going to start thinking that you've abandoned him," Allen said.

Reagan looked up from her computer and scowled. "He is not. I went home at nine last night."

"For how long?"

She sighed. "I woke up at four-thirty and couldn't get back to sleep so I decided to go ahead and come in to work. With the new attacks in Indiana and Ohio, we honestly can't afford to sleep right now."

"Don't forget West Virginia," Allen said.

"What?"

Agent Williams nodded. "Heard it on the radio driving in. Morgantown, West Virginia got hit sometime either overnight or early this morning. Four dead and nine hospitalized so far."

Reagan picked up her laptop as if she was going to throw it across the room but then thought better of the situation. She gently placed the computer back on the conference room table and ran her fingers through her long hair. "Okay," Reagan said. "West Virginia, too. But, even adding that in, I think I've got something."

Allen's eyes lit up. The pair hadn't had a solid lead in days.

"What?"

"Not what," Agent White corrected, "who. I took your map idea and entered it all into my computer. I was then able to narrow down where our guy is likely coming from, based on travel distance between the attack locations. Eastern Kentucky and West Virginia are our best bets." Reagan started typing into her laptop as she spoke. "I ran searches of people who live in those areas to see if anything turned up."

She spun her laptop around on her desk to show Allen the screen. "That's Raymond Van Klopp. He lives near a small town in Kentucky called Olive Hill. The guy would be completely off-the-grid if not for his 'all government is tyranny' blog. Apparently, he hand writes the posts and then mails them to some college kid who maintains the website."

Allen wasn't following the storyline. "What does an anarchist blog have to do with the FEB Killer?"

Reagan grinned. "Did I mention Mr. Van Klopp also has a Bachelor's and Master's in Biomedical Engineering from Morehead State?"

Agent Williams returned his partner's smile. "What do you say we pay Mr. Van Klopp a visit?"

Allen turned to go ask their boss for travel permission when his phone rang.

"Williams," he answered. There was a few seconds pause while Allen listened to the person on the other end of the line.

"Seriously?" he replied. "And where was this? West Virginia?" A longer pause. "Okay, yeah. Box it up and get it to the lab here at Headquarters as fast as you can. Great work . . . this just might be the break we need."

Allen hung up his phone and turned back around to face Reagan. A trademark smile lit up his face.

"What is it?" Reagan asked.

"Change of plans. Forensics found three wads of dissolvable paper just inside the fence at the water treatment plant in Morgantown. Workers said they weren't there yesterday and have no idea where they came from." Allen's smile spread wider on his face. "I think he screwed up. I mean, I think he or she screwed up. Maybe this fancy paper is how the killer is getting the bacteria into the water."

Reagan looked at her partner skeptically. "What, by making giant bacteria-laden spit balls and throwing them over the fence?"

"Sure."

"You seriously think that somebody with the know how to make a new bacteria from scratch is going to resort to something as bush-league as that?"

"Maybe," replied Allen. "Why not, if it works?"

****

Scientists in the forensics lab at the FBI's Headquarters quickly tired of the two field agents hovering in the corner of the room. Reagan and Allen had camped out in the laboratory and were pestering the technicians about the paper found in West Virginia.

"Really," the staff supervisor finally said, "we'll call you when we find something. It might be a while. Surely there are other things you could be doing?"

Allen and Reagan glanced back and forth at each other. He shrugged. "Not really. We're kind of stuck right now. There's one suspect we're going to check out, but this is a much more solid lead."

"Okay, fine," the supervisor replied. "But please just stay in the corner and be quiet so we can do our work."

Forty-five minutes later, the lab tech raised his head from a microscope. "Alright, you two. It's confirmed: the bacteria on the paper is a match for that in the other attacks. It looks like this is your delivery mechanism."

Agents Williams and White both smiled, resisting the urge to give each other high fives.

This is huge, thought Reagan. *So huge.* New investigation ideas immediately began running through her mind. *We need to canvas all of the other water treatment plants and interview employees to see if they found any paper like this. And we need to go back over all of the security footage that we have. There has to be at least one shot of these little bacteria balls being tossed over the fences.*

Allen broke into Reagan's thoughts. "This is great," he said to the technicians. "Such a big break." Looking over at his partner, he added: "ready to go see about that guy in Kentucky?"

THIRTY-SEVEN

Assistant Deputy Director Molina approved the trip to Kentucky without hesitation. However, upon placing a call to the Morehead, Kentucky field office, Agents Williams and White learned they would have to wait until the following day to travel. A local law enforcement official was advised to serve as a middleman between the federal investigators and Mr. Van Klopp, and the earliest the local sheriff would be able to escort them was Sunday afternoon. Something about a softball tournament and church.

The FBI's private pilots knew Reagan and Allen by name now, and happily said "Welcome aboard, Agents White and Williams" when the partners hopped yet another flight - this time to the heart of Appalachia in eastern Kentucky.

The plane trip hadn't taken long at all, but the two agents were now closing in on an hour of drive time. *And we haven't seen a soul for the last thirty minutes. Reagan wasn't kidding when she said this guy lived off the grid,* Allen thought, his words rattling in time with the bumpy road.

"Jus' a couple more minutes, y'all," said the sheriff driving the car.

This Van Klopp guy must really be something if we need a local escort, Reagan thought. She half expected the suspect to walk out of his cabin wearing a Ku Klux Klan robe and hood.

Another ten minutes later, the sheriff turned off of what Reagan had thought was an unpaved street and onto a truly unpaved, red clay packed, pothole-filled road. It didn't even really qualify as a road in her opinion. More like a path cleared wide enough to fit a car.

The sheriff - Dave was his name ("folks just call me Sheriff Dave") - slowed the car to a stop and leaned around in his seat. "We're on Van Klopp's land now. Y'all just stick behind me and let me do the talkin', aw right? Raymond don't take too kindly to visitors. 'Specially ones not from 'round here."

Both FBI agents nodded their heads in agreement. Allen now knew why the field agents suggested a local expert. He could barely understand what Sheriff Dave was saying, and Allen figured that Van Klopp's accent was likely even worse.

Sheriff Dave put the car back in drive and proceeded deeper into the suspect's property. After a long stretch of 'road' surrounded by tall pine trees, the three law enforcement officers reached a clearing in the woods. In the middle of the clearing was a beautiful log cabin, obviously built from scratch with exceptional attention to detail.

"Wow," Reagan said.

"Yeah," the sheriff answered. "Ray coulda been a great architect if he wanted to. We actually went to school together, him and me. First through twelfth grade. Real smart guy. Super smart. Got those degrees from Morehead but then never did anythin' with 'em. Ray always had that chip on his shoulder. Legend 'round here is that Ray's momma went crazy when he was a baby and they took her away. Folks say that's why he hates the government so much."

"Is it true?" Allen asked.

"About his momma? Dunno," Dave shrugged. He then opened his car door, stepped out, and put his sheriff's hat back on his balding head. "Now 'member, y'all let me do the talkin'."

The two FBI agents walked behind the sheriff as they approached the cabin.

"How can he not know if that story is true?" whispered Reagan.

"Beats me," Allen whispered back. "This whole place has a 'Deliverance' feel to it to me."

Reagan's reply was interrupted by a loud commotion as the cabin's front door swung open and a middle-aged man with a full head of shock white hair emerged.

With his shotgun, Reagan noted. *At least he left his cape and hood inside.*

"Waddaya want, Dave?" the man called out.

The sheriff didn't seem fazed. "Oh come on, Ray. Put the gun down. We ain't here to arrest you."

Van Klopp eyed his visitors warily, sizing up any potential threat. Finally, he acceded to the sheriff's order and placed his gun across the arms of a rocking chair.

"Who are they?" he asked, nodding in the direction of the agents in their nearly matching black suits.

Sheriff Dave glanced over his shoulder. "Jus' a couple of FBI agents down from Washington. They wanna ask you some questions." Dave paused. "You gonna invite us in or what?"

Van Klopp shook his head in the negative. "House is a mess. Shirley's gone visitin' her parents, and Lord knows I cain't take care of myself." He gestured to the row of rocking chairs on the front porch. "Y'all can sit up here, I guess. Leave yer firearms in the car," he added.

Much to Reagan's surprise, Sheriff Dave began to undo the buckle on his gun holster. "Are you crazy?" she asked.

The sheriff shrugged. "His property, his rules. We don't have a warrant. We're his guests."

"Well," Allen said, "as his guest I would feel a lot more comfortable if my host would put his own gun back inside."

Dave nodded. "Fair 'nuff."

When the gun issue was resolved and the four adults were seated on Van Klopp's porch, Sheriff Dave again took the lead in the conversation.

"Ray, this is Agent Reagan White and Agent Allen Williams from the FBI. They're investigatin' that flesh-eatin' bacteria thing."

"I get my water fresh from a well out back," Van Klopp replied. "Don't gotta worry 'bout that."

Unbeknownst to the homeowner, his first response made him look even guiltier in the eyes of his visitors.

"We understand you hold degrees in Biomedical Engineering from Morehead State University," Allen said.

"Yeah. So?"

"And that you aren't particularly fond of the government," Reagan added.

"What's yer point, darlin'?"

She didn't pull any punches. "Did you poison the water?"

Van Klopp's stone cold face began to crack. The lines by his eyes crinkled and soon his booming laughter filled the woods. When the laughing subsided, he said:

"Y'all came all the way down here to ask me that? Why on Earth would I do that, hon'? All that's doin' is killin' innocent Americans. If I was gonna kill somebody, it'd be somebody guilty. One of them damn politicians ruinin' everythin' that made this country great." He paused and stuck an index finger up in front of him as a correction. "And I said 'if' I was gonna kill somebody. Don't y'all go accusin' me of terrorist threats or nothin' like that."

A silence descended upon the porch. Reagan could hear crickets chirping in the woods nearby. *Crap*, she thought. *I believe him. I'll get IT to run a check on his bank and phone records, but we probably came all the way out here for nothing.*

****

"Who is Shirley?" Reagan asked once the law enforcement crew was back in the sheriff's car and headed toward the main road.

"Who?" Dave asked.

"Shirley. Van Klopp said someone named Shirley was visiting her parents. Is that his housekeeper?"

The sheriff laughed. "Well, I guess that's one thing you could call her. I think she'd like homemaker better. Shirley is

Ray's wife." He shook his head and whistled. "Sure caused a fuss 'round here when those two got married."

"Why?" Allen asked.

"Shirley's black. Light-skinned, you know - what people used to call high yella - but still black. Lot a folks 'round here still don't like the idea of race mixin'. Course, Ray never really cared much about what other people thought."

"Good for him," Allen replied, his opinion on Van Klopp having done a complete one-eighty in the past hour.

Reagan, for her part, remained quiet. A feeling of guilt settled in the pit of her stomach. *Stereotyping only gets you in trouble*, she scolded herself. *Who's the racist now?*

THIRTY-EIGHT

President Hughes' well-publicized summit with the Joint Terrorism Task Force and FBI chiefs took place on that same Sunday afternoon, conveniently right after the morning talk shows had time to tout the event and how proactive the president was being in trying to find the FEB Killer.

"There's nothing more we in this White House can do to find the guy," Daniel Bader told his deputies before the meeting. "That's up to law enforcement. What we can do is limit the damage this does to President Hughes' reputation. He will not go down in history as the deadly outbreak president. At least not if we can help it."

FBI Director Jack Leyton, Counterterrorism Task Force Chief Bill Smalley, the Speaker of the House, and the Senate Majority Leader all descended upon the West Wing at one o'clock. The men and their various aides took seats around a large table in the Roosevelt Room, the same room where President Hughes had honored Dr. Isaac Carlson and his team for their excellent work on the SuperAIDS case. A projector screen pulled down over one of the room's ornate walls was flashing a 'waiting for signal' sign.

"Thank you for coming in here on a Sunday," the president began. Motioning to the wall, he said: "the two FBI agents in charge of the investigation are supposed to be on that screen right now."

"We're working on it, sir," his Chief of Staff replied. "Agent White and Agent Williams are in a small town in Kentucky so we're having some trouble getting a secure line out to them."

"Well then let's just get started and they can jump in whenever it gets fixed," Hughes declared. "Smalley, give me a Joint Terrorism Task Force status report."

A rail-thin man with a shaved head and thick, wire-rimmed glasses coughed to clear his throat. "Yes sir, Mr.

President. As you know, the FBI is taking lead on this particular incident. But all of the Homeland Security component groups - ATF, ICE, Customs, etcetera - as well as state and local law enforcement are providing backup support and filling in any logistical gaps with the Bureau."

"Is there anything you need to do your job that you're not currently getting?" The question came from the Speaker of the House.

"No sir. We have access to a wide variety of investigatory tools. I can't think of anything where my agents say 'oh, if we only had this'." He issued a wry grin. "Within the limits of the law and the Constitution, anyway."

The elected officials in the room nodded. "What about you," the Speaker asked, looking at the FBI Director. "Do you need anything?"

"Well, sir, now that you mention it," Jack Leyton replied, "the name of the person behind the attacks would be nice."

Laughter filled the room and broke some of the tension being felt by the nation's leaders. The death and illness of dozens of citizens was an ongoing tragedy, and it certainly didn't reflect well on the politicians' crisis management skills.

At that moment the projector screen began to flash, made a few hissing noises, and then finally turned on to show the faces of the two aforementioned FBI agents.

"Hello? Can you hear us?" asked President Hughes.

"Yes sir, Mr. President. We can both hear and see you," Allen answered. He and Reagan were seated behind Sheriff Dave's desk in the Olive Hill Police Station.

Director Leyton recognized his agents. "Introduce yourselves," he said. "And then give us an update on the status of the investigation."

Allen nodded. "Yes sir. My name is Agent Allen Williams and this is my partner Agent Reagan White. Agent White is very experienced with what we call field work, or investigating unsolved cases. I typically spend more time in the counterterrorism branch working on ways to prevent future attacks."

"The investigation is obviously still ongoing," Reagan said. "We have a few strong leads and a very competent team of assistants helping in the search. We're confident that we will be able to locate the FEB Killer and bring him or her - or them - to justice."

"So where do we go from here?" asked the president.

"Well, sir," Allen answered, "in the immediate future Agent Williams and I will fly back to Washington. At this point all we can personally do is try to narrow down a list of suspects and look for any clues in the towns and cities that have been hit. However, at our suggestion the FBI has issued a directive that every water treatment facility be placed under guard by either local police or federal agents."

"We can send in the National Guard if need be," the Speaker of the House said.

President Hughes nodded. "Let's leave it up to each state, but if they need the extra manpower then yeah, I definitely think this qualifies as a state of emergency."

"Whatever you think is best, sir," Reagan said. "Part of the directive also included instructions for the treatment facilities to cover any outdoor water containers with a tarp or netting of some sort to prevent the bacteria from being launched into them. We may not know who the killer is yet, but there are definite concrete steps we can take to prevent any more attacks."

"Excellent," replied the Senate Majority Leader. "Good work, you two."

"One more thing," Reagan added. "There shouldn't be any more attacks until next weekend. All of the outbreaks so far have occurred Friday through Sunday, and we have no reason to believe that the perpetrator will change his tactics."

"He has a job," the FBI Director said.

"Beg your pardon?" President Hughes asked.

"That's your conclusion, am I correct?" Director Leyton said to his subordinates. "That the suspect has a regular day job?"

Reagan nodded. "Yes sir it is. There's no other reason why he or she would only hit on the weekends. We are very confident in our conclusion that the person we're looking for has a regular, nine-to-five, Monday-to-Friday job."

"That means someone has to know him. Work with him," Daniel Bader added. "This isn't about law enforcement agencies getting more resources. What we need more than anything right now is for civilian Americans to step up their vigilance. I mean, hell, the Unabomber's own brother turned him in. That's what's going to crack this case," the Chief of Staff surmised. "A tip."

"You may be right about that," Allen replied.

****

While President Hughes and his team met to discuss the bacterial outbreaks and the so-called FEB Killer, the man they were hunting for sat comfortably at his kitchen table less than thirty minutes away.

"Where do we want to go next, hmm?"

Joseph had his large paper Atlas spread before him on the table. Nothing was marked; no notes on travel plans or drop sites. *I'm not stupid enough to leave evidence like that*, the doctor thought. He knew his exact routes the past three weekends, though. First had been a short trip, a trial run of sorts that only included one drop in Halliston, Pennsylvania.

Things swung into high gear after that, Joseph knew, his finger tracing the roads he took to get from Bethesda to Atlanta, and then back up through Tennessee and Virginia. Dr. Carlson had been careful to take a different return path and make drops farther west so that it wouldn't look like he was based out of anywhere on the East Coast.

And it worked, Joseph thought with a smile, since news reports were now saying that the government believed the FEB Killer was from somewhere in the Kentucky, Ohio, or West Virginia area. *Appalachia: breeding ground for idiots, racists, and people who want to overthrow the government.* Joseph laughed. "They really couldn't have profiled me any worse."

He took a long sip from a glass of water that only he could know was safe. "Last weekend definitely helped with that misdirection. Even if driving all the way out to Indiana was a pain in the ass." Joseph paused for another drink. "Sure beats Colorado, though," he added, remembering the first drop location for his SuperAIDS virus.

"And speaking of Colorado," Joseph said, returning his attention to the map, "where do I want to hit next? I know I can't make any drops this upcoming weekend because I'm speaking at that conference in Boston."

Or could I? he thought. *I would already be up there. Could probably disguise a petri dish or two of bacteria in my bags. Yeah, that could be good.*

The idea of a New England drop was appealing to Dr. Carlson for several reasons. At the top of the list was the fact that he already knew the area fairly well from his time at Harvard. Joseph even knew the first spot he would hit: a large reservoir a few miles from Harvard's main campus that provided drinking water to the city of Cambridge. Having run on the path hundreds of times that looped around the pond, Joseph knew security was extremely lax. *Hell, I wouldn't even need the potato gun*, he thought. *Just go for a jog and chuck it over the fence.*

A second later, though, Joseph knew he couldn't pick New England.

"Anyone plotting the outbreak locations on a map would see that Baltimore and DC are right in the middle of it all. Plus my speech at the conference would publicly put me in the same vicinity while the attacks occurred. No," Joseph shook his head, "you've gotta go west, young man."

Dr. Carlson's finger traced his next line of attack on the Atlas. Out to Texas, then back east with drops in Arkansas, Missouri, and Kentucky. *No outbreaks this weekend will make people think it might be over*, Joseph thought with a smile. *Then, the weekend after that, I'll strike back with a vengeance.*

"We can do this one and be done, Joe," he told himself. "We only have enough bacteria left for four drops." He smiled. "Then we can sit back and watch the carnage. Or maybe even step in and save a few lives." Dr. Carlson laughed and leaned back in his chair. "I can see the headlines now: Hero Doctor Does It Again."

THIRTY-NINE

The following Saturday afternoon, Reagan found herself working, yet again, at FBI headquarters. She and Allen hadn't taken any time off since the case started twenty days ago, and the stress and strain was starting to eat away at the veteran agent. *No pun intended*, Reagan thought. The worst part, she recognized, was the fact that they seemed no farther along in the investigation. Searches of the other outbreak locations hadn't turned up any more bacteria paper, and the list of potential suspects was still a mile long. Agent White knew she was running out of ideas.

The conference table where she was working shook a little bit, and Reagan looked up to see Allen's phone vibrating across the table. Since her partner was still down the hall getting a bite to eat, and knowing that the call might be important, Reagan leaned forward across the table to pick up the still buzzing phone.

"Agent Williams' phone," she said, not bothering to first check Caller ID.

"Hello? Allen?"

Agent White didn't recognize the woman's voice on the other end of the line. Holding the phone away from her ear, Reagan looked down at the screen to see who the caller was: 'Mom'. *Oops*, she thought.

Gathering her bearings, Reagan finally replied: "no ma'am. Agent Williams is out of the room at the moment. May I help you?"

"Who am I talking to?" the mom asked.

"I'm sorry. Reagan White. I'm Allen's partner on the FEB Killer case."

"Oh!" Mrs. Williams exclaimed. "I knew he was working with another agent, I just didn't know who. I'm Becky, Allen's mom."

"Hi," Reagan responded, not sure if she should be happy or upset that Allen hadn't told his mother about her.

The son in question chose that moment to walk back into the conference room holding two coffee cups.

"Here he is now," Reagan said before taking a cup of coffee from Allen's hand and replacing it with his phone. "It's your mom," she whispered.

"Mom, hi. What's up?"

"She sounds nice," was Mrs. Williams' reply.

Allen sighed, glancing over at Reagan to see if she was paying attention. Luckily, it looked like his partner had gone back to reviewing files. "What can I do for you, Mom?"

"Funny you should ask. You can come to Sunday dinner tomorrow. And bring Reagan. I want to meet her."

"I can't," Allen said. "I've told you a hundred times, Mom. The entire team is working around the clock until we catch this guy."

The former elementary school teacher wasn't taking no for an answer. "You haven't been to Sunday dinner in two months, so don't give me that important case nonsense. Plus you have to eat at some point. And taking an hour out of your Sunday to relax and rejuvenate will help you do a better job. Recharge your batteries."

Allen rolled his eyes. He knew his mom had him beat. "Fine, I'll come. But I'm sure Agent White is too busy."

Reagan looked up when she heard her name. "Too busy for what?"

Agent Williams knew Reagan had him beat too. "Sunday dinner at my parents' house. They live in McLean. My mom wants you to come."

Allen watched as Reagan tried and failed to hide the adorable little grin spreading across her face. *Stop it*, he told himself. *She's not adorable. She's your partner*.

"I guess we do have to eat at some point," Reagan said. "And it would be horribly rude of me to say no to a personal invitation from your mom."

"I'll take that as a yes?"

"Yes," answered Reagan, not bothering to hide the grin now.

"Okay, Mom," Allen said into his cell phone. "You win. We'll be there."

FORTY

It didn't matter how many times Reagan made the trip from her apartment to the affluent suburb of McLean or the adjacent popular shopping area of Tyson's Corner, Virginia. She never got tired of the beauty of the drive. Tree-lined George Washington Parkway wrapped and wound its way along the banks of the Potomac River, giving motorists breathtaking views of the national monuments and cliff-side Chain Bridge Road mansions.

"I love this drive," Allen said, mimicking Reagan's thoughts. He had picked her up at her apartment and the pair was now on their way to Sunday dinner at his parents' house. "Especially this part," he added. "Right . . . now."

Allen pointed across the river to his alma mater, Georgetown University. "Best four years of my life."

"Everyone I know who went there talks about Georgetown like it's a slice of Heaven on Earth."

Allen smiled. "That's because it is."

Reagan looked over at him. "I don't understand that kind of visceral reaction to a college. The sports' teams? Maybe. But the school itself? I mean, don't get me wrong, I enjoyed my time at UCF. But it's not like it became a part of my soul or anything."

Her partner shrugged his shoulders and gave an impish grin. "Should've gone to Georgetown."

Twenty minutes later, after Reagan was forced to listen to more college glory days stories from Allen, the agents pulled into the driveway of a large two-story colonial.

"This is where you grew up?" Agent White asked, shocked.

"Yeah . . . why?"

"It's like a postcard," she gushed. "Or a Norman Rockwell painting."

Allen took a minute to see his childhood home through Reagan's eyes. "Yeah, I guess it is pretty nice. I never really took the time to notice."

Reagan rolled her eyes as she got out of the car. *Typical rich kid*, she thought.

****

Sunday Dinner at the Williams household was actually a late lunch, starting with cocktails at the two o'clock hour. When Allen and Reagan walked in at 2:15, Doug Williams had already poured himself a stiff scotch and was positioned behind a grill in the backyard.

The cookie-cutter image was completed when Allen's mom, a petite woman with close-cropped brown hair, emerged from the house carrying a tray of iced tea. Becky Williams set the tray down on a perfectly appointed table and then turned to embrace her son.

"I'm so happy you came!" she crooned. Releasing Allen from a bear hug, his mom switched her focus to Agent White.

"And you must be Reagan. It's so great to meet you. And let me just say," Mrs. Williams added, "you are by far the prettiest partner my son has ever had at the FBI."

Reagan shook her hostess' hand and smiled. "From what I heard, all of his other partners have been men."

Allen's dad chimed in from the grill. "Don't ruin a good story with facts, Agent White."

The four adults laughed and continued a pleasant conversation until the food was ready a few minutes later. All the while, Reagan kept thinking how lucky Allen was to have grown up in a household like this one. *This is what I always wanted*, she thought. *The closeness, the joking around. Even when they push each other's buttons . . . just the fact that they know each other well enough to know which buttons to push. A solid family. They're great.*

Seated at the table outside and enjoying the unseasonably cool, dry late June afternoon, Reagan was also pleasantly surprised by Mrs. Williams' friendly and engaging nature. Agent White didn't have much experience being around rich people, and they usually made her feel uncomfortable. *Not with Allen's mom, though,* she thought.

The 'great' label soon fell away from her assessment of her partner's dad, though. The elder Mr. Williams was already three whiskeys into the afternoon and didn't appear to have much of a filter as far as conversation topics were concerned.

"So the serial killer is still making you all look like idiots, huh?"

"Doug!" his wife hissed. "That's not true and certainly not appropriate."

"Oh they can take it," the lobbyist answered back. "They're big, tough FBI agents." He paused. "But seriously, son, how long are you going to let this maniac run free?"

Allen gritted his teeth and glared at the plate in front of him, clearly seething inside but equally unwilling to challenge his father.

"We're working as hard as we can, Mr. Williams," Reagan replied. "And Allen has been doing a great job. This is just a very difficult case and a very difficult disease."

"About that disease," the balding man said with another sip of scotch, "the news keeps saying it's a bacterial disease. But isn't it really more like a poison?"

"What do you mean?" asked Allen.

"They die so fast," his dad responded. "I heard that doctors and police can't even get a statement out of them. Hell, from what I've heard, they're lucky if they even get to the hospital before they keel over." Doug Williams paused. "It's the perfect crime, really."

The son reluctantly nodded his head. "You're right, Dad. It is the perfect crime. That's why we're having so much trouble with it." He ran a frustrated hand through his hair. "I mean, this is what I do. I try to find weaknesses. Try to decide where I would attack if I were a terrorist. This guy - or guys, or girls - this crime . . . it's perfect. The security cameras at the drop spots aren't showing anything useful. No signs of breaking and entering so no possibility of evidence left behind. The paper left at the plant in West Virginia is the only break we've gotten. And sure," Allen continued, "there's a trail, so we have somewhat of a geographical idea, but that's still millions of potential suspects." He sighed. "*Millions*."

"So, what you're saying is, you're screwed," his dad concluded.

At that moment, sensing an impending battle between her husband and son, Becky Williams broke into the conversation. "Why don't we talk about something aside from work? I'm sure Allen and Reagan would appreciate a break from all of that."

Doug Williams smiled, a mischievous glint entering his eyes. "Sure. How about a childhood story or two? After all," he went on, "I feel it's my duty as a parent to embarrass my son at least a little bit in front of his work colleague."

The father shifted his tone ever so slightly at the end of the sentence, just enough to let Allen know that he didn't buy the 'we're only work colleagues' line.

"No, Dad. Don't."

Becky Williams jumped to her son's defense. "Really, Doug, that's not necessary."

But Allen's father was now nursing his fourth whiskey and wouldn't listen. "Oh come on, it'll be funny. The story is more cute than anything else."

Allen sighed heavily and buried his head in his hands.

"Every summer," Mr. Williams began, "when Al and his sister were young, we would go on vacation to the beach. Usually somewhere in the Carolinas." He paused long enough for another sip of whiskey. "We went to dinner one night at a marina-side restaurant, you know the kind of place where boats are always coming and going and everything reeks of fish. Anyway, we're there, and little Allen here got bored. What were you at the time, like thirteen?"

"Twelve," Allen groaned. He knew what was coming.

"Twelve. Right. So he leaves the table and goes and starts walking around the marina looking at the boats. Now this was back when that song 'Macarena' was really big. You know which one I'm talking about Ray?"

"It's Reagan, Dad," the son corrected.

"I can give your *colleague* a nickname if I want to," Mr. Williams retorted, the alcohol flowing freely through his brain. "You know that song, though?"

"Yes sir, I do," Reagan nodded.

"Right. So the Macarena comes on, and Fred Astaire here starts doing that stupid arm-turning dance that went along with it. The whole front of the restaurant was windows, so everyone got to watch his little performance."

Reagan tried to muffle her laughter.

"No, go ahead, laugh," Allen said. "The song ended and I turned around to see the entire restaurant clapping for me."

The laughter burst through as Reagan doubled over in her chair in a fit of giggles.

"I was mortified, thank you. But I'm glad my humiliation could entertain you."

"I'm sorry, I'm sorry," Reagan said. Then, to more laughter: "No, I'm not. That's hilarious."

Allen rolled his eyes and stood up. "I think now would be a good time to do the dishes. I'll be in the kitchen if you need me."

****

Mrs. Williams found her older child at the sink in her kitchen, furiously scrubbing an already sparkling clean dish.

"You break it you buy it," she said gently.

Allen stopped scrubbing. "We both know you can't buy these plates anymore. You've been telling me since before I could walk that they were priceless family heirlooms."

Becky smiled. "That's not what I meant."

The son sighed. "I know. But I'm not in the mood to talk, okay?"

"Okay. I'll talk. You listen."

Agent Williams rolled his eyes and resumed the dish cleaning.

"It seems to me," his mom said, "that you got a tad bit embarrassed by your dad telling that story. Am I right?"

"Maybe."

"It also seems to me that I usually hear all about your work colleagues, but I haven't heard anything about Reagan. You tell me about the beer-bellied beat cops, the computer science code breakers, and the polyglot sons of globe-trotting diplomats. But I don't get to hear so much as a word about the lovely, talented, not altogether unattractive Agent White." She paused. When Allen didn't reply, Mrs. Williams said: "honey, put down the plate and the brush and look at me for a minute."

Allen did as he was told.

"The last time you kept a girl a secret from your father and me, you dated her for three years and were head-over-heels in love."

"Reagan's not a girl. She's my partner on this case. That's all."

"Are you sure about that?" Becky Williams pressed. "It looked to me like there might be something going on between you two."

"There's nothing going on. Trust me."

"Okay, okay. I trust you. I'll back off." The mother turned around to walk back outside, then stopped. "I only brought it up because Reagan seems pretty great."

"That's because she is," Allen replied.

His mom nodded, turned back around, and left the kitchen. Her mission was complete. Her suspicions confirmed. *He's crazy about this girl.*

FORTY-ONE

The morning after their family dinner in the suburb of McLean, Reagan and Allen found themselves back in their downtown DC office building. The two agents in charge of one of the biggest cases in recent FBI history had long ago commandeered the only conference room on the twelfth floor and didn't let anyone else inside. When they left, the doors were locked - even to the janitorial staff. Empty takeout containers now shared space with highly sensitive government memos and files.

"Do you think it's done?" Reagan asked in a whisper.

Allen glanced over at his partner and shook his head. "No. And why are you whispering? Afraid you might jinx it if it was over?"

Agent White glared back. "Maybe."

Allen issued a short laugh. "No, sorry," he repeated. "I don't think it's over. It's true that there weren't any attacks this weekend, but I don't think somebody like the FEB Killer would only do three weekends and then quit. Especially when he or she is getting away with it. The beefed-up security at each water treatment facility and the nets over the open pools certainly help us, but again . . . this guy or girl isn't going to give up that easily."

"Yeah," Reagan sighed. "I guess you're right."

"White! Williams!" A bellowing voice from down the hall broke through the otherwise quiet twelfth floor.

Reagan and Allen collectively rolled their eyes and shook their heads.

"We're being summoned," Reagan said. The two agents stood up from the conference room table and made their way out of the makeshift office, down the hall, and to the location of their summoner.

Allen rapped his knuckles against Bruce Molina's office door before he entered the room, followed by Reagan.

"This won't take long," their boss began, "or at least I hope it won't given the mountain of paperwork I have to do today." Noticing that both of the junior agents were still standing, the Assistant Deputy Director motioned to the chairs in front of his desk. "Have a seat, you two. No need to stand at attention."

Agents Williams and White quietly obliged and sat down.

"Look," Molina continued, "I know you're busy and I know the kind of hours you've been pulling while working on this case. But I've got everyone from the Director to the damn White House Chief of Staff calling my office every five minutes asking when we're going to solve this thing and catch this sonofabitch. So where are we? Give me something I can take back to them and say 'look, here, progress.'"

Reagan and Allen glanced sideways at each other, a silent question of who should talk first. Reagan took the lead.

"Well, sir, to be honest . . . 'progress' is such a complicated word."

"Make it uncomplicated," her boss ordered.

"Let's start with the positives then," Reagan said. "Based on the location of the seven outbreaks, we've narrowed down a general geographical area for the search. The FEB Killer is likely based somewhere in the eastern Kentucky or southern West Virginia region."

"Okay," Molina nodded. "What else?"

"We figured out how the water is being poisoned," said Allen. "As I'm sure you know, some wads of paper were found at a water treatment plant in Morgantown, West Virginia. Forensics examined them and found large amounts of the deadly bacteria. We believe the killer is exposing the paper to the bacteria, possibly soaking it in it, and then somehow launching the balls of paper over the fences at the treatment facilities."

"How is that not being caught on video?"

"The drop sites were chosen strategically, sir," Reagan explained. "Some were in rural areas without cameras, and those in cities are located directly adjacent to busy streets. With the right equipment, it would be entirely possible to literally do a drive-by shooting. Just send the bacteria out your window as you pass by the plant in your car."

"You're kidding."

"Unfortunately not, sir."

"And as far as actual suspects go?" Molina asked.

Reagan and Allen exchanged looks again.

"We went down to Kentucky to talk to one guy," Allen replied. "It was a dead end though."

"We're currently looking through police records and talking to universities in our search zone to see who might have the knowledge necessary to make the bacteria plus the motive or desire to do something like this."

"Alright," the boss said, nodding his head. "That should be enough to keep the brass at bay for a few more days. But seriously, you two, we need this one solved. Don't think that just because this weekend was outbreak free that we're somehow in the clear now."

The agents issued a collective "yes sir."

Molina dismissed them with a wave. "You're done."

Before Reagan and Allen could exit his office, though, the Assistant Deputy Director added: "Williams, hang back a minute."

Allen shrugged his shoulders at Reagan to indicate that he didn't know what their boss wanted. After she left, he said "yes sir?"

"Close the door."

Allen did as he was told.

Bruce Molina took a deep breath. "Sit back down for a minute, son."

Son? thought Allen. *He's definitely never called me that before.*

"Look, as you can probably tell, I'm not at all comfortable talking about this. And it's not a conversation I've had to have before. But it needs to be done, so hear me out."

"Okay . . . " Allen shifted nervously in his chair. *Is he going to fire me?*

"Reagan White is my best field agent," Molina began. "She's been working cases for twelve years now and nobody does the job better than her. Nobody. To be honest with you, she could have my job or just about any other position in the Bureau that she wanted; all she would have to do is ask. Everybody knows that if Agent White is on a case it's going to be solved." He paused. "Do you understand what I'm saying?"

"Uhh . . . not really."

The boss ran his fingers through his hair. "What I'm trying to say is that she doesn't need any distractions, alright? Agent White is married to the job, for better or worse. Everyone in the major crimes division knows her and respects her and we all kind of look out for her. She's everybody's daughter or sister, depending on their age."

Williams furrowed his brow in confusion. "I agree, sir. I think Reagan is, well, she's great. She's amazing. I just don't know why you're telling me all of this."

Molina sighed. "You've known Agent White for how long now?"

"About three weeks."

"And you've had a thing for her for how long?" Molina asked.

"A thing?"

"Don't play dumb, Williams. A thing. A crush. You like her."

This time it was Allen's turn to take a deep breath. He slouched back in the chair. *No point in lying about it.* "Yes sir, I do. I have. Pretty much since Day One."

"I'm telling you all of this," the Assistant Deputy Director said, "because I can't afford to have my best field agent get distracted. I know she seems tough and trust me, ninety-nine percent of the time Agent White is a force to be reckoned with. But she doesn't date a lot. And by 'not a lot' I mean 'at all'. She gets shy. It's amazing - you take away the badge and the all-powerful crime fighter morphs into this timid wallflower." He paused. "All I'm saying is be careful. And if you hurt her, I swear I'll kill you. I'll kill you and make it look like an accident."

"Yes sir," Allen nodded. "I understand. I won't. Hurt her, that is. I will be careful."

"Alright, good. Now get out of here. And don't you dare tell her I said any of this to you."

FORTY-TWO

The next several days passed without much fanfare for Reagan and Allen. The two agents continued to work around the clock, interviewing victims and chasing down leads that always finished at a dead end. Water treatment plant workers had alibis. The ones that didn't had no motive, no financial advantage, and zero ties to any terrorist groups.

"This isn't working," Reagan said one afternoon.

Allen, seated across from her at their conference table, looked up from his computer. "What isn't working?"

"This," she replied, gesturing around the room with her hands. "Every day we spend sifting through these suspect lists and talking to victims who know absolutely nothing is another day that the FEB Killer gets to roam free and plot more attacks. We need to change tactics. Change something."

Agent Williams stood up from his chair and motioned for his partner to follow him. "Come on. There are some guys we should talk to."

Reagan didn't know what guys Allen was talking about, but she followed him anyway. More out of curiosity and a desire to get out of the stuffy conference room than anything else.

"Where are we going?" she asked.

"Just wait. You'll see."

A quick elevator ride and a short walk down a hall later, the two investigators arrived at their destination in the basement of the FBI Headquarters. A sign on the door read 'Profiling.'

Allen knocked but didn't wait for a response before he opened the door and walked into a large office. "Hey fellas. Remember me?"

Several heads popped up from behind cubicle walls and smiled in greeting to Agent Williams. "What's up bro?" one asked. "Where you been?"

"New case, man. They moved me up to the twelfth floor for a while."

Turning to Reagan, Allen explained: "these guys do all of our profiling for us. The running joke is that the office is in the basement because the brass doesn't want the public to know that we discriminate on the basis of race and religion all the time. Isn't that right, Caleb?"

The man who spoke earlier grinned and walked out from behind his cubicle to shake hands with the visitors. "Yep," Caleb replied. "Race, religion, country of origin, hell I discriminate on the basis of gender and sexuality too. All day, every day."

Reagan didn't see what was so funny about the conversation. "No offense, but wasn't it profiling that led police to say the DC sniper was a single white male? When it ended up being two African-American males?"

The profiler didn't appreciate the reference. "An exception to the rule," he said curtly.

"So, listen," Allen said, trying to change subjects, "I've got a confession to make."

"Sure," the profiler said, brushing off Reagan's comments with a smile. "What's on your heart, bro?"

What's on your heart, bro? Reagan thought. *What is this, group therapy?*

"We're in a real tight spot with this FEB Killer case," Allen continued. "The list of possible suspects is just too long for us to make any real progress on it, even with all of the help we've been getting from field offices around the country. Can you maybe give us a heads up on what kind of person we should be looking for?"

Caleb grinned and shook his head in disbelief. "This thing has been going on for how long? And you're just now coming to see us? But hey, better late than never. Especially if you take a look at the memos we've been sending out about serial killers and what traits to look for." He gestured toward a small, round table in a corner where they could all sit. "But I'd be happy to do a little crash course with you now."

"That'd be great," Reagan said.

The profiling expert wasted no time and jumped right in to his explanation. "Common knowledge and centuries of experience tells us that most serial killers are two things: male and working alone. The minute you throw in a partner or two or three, you're adding the potential for somebody to screw up or turn state's evidence or whatever. So you're going to be looking primarily for men with a reputation for being loners. The vast majority of serial killers are also white and in their thirties and forties." Caleb stopped to look at Allen and Reagan. "You two should know all of this already."

"Okay then," Allen said, "tell us something we don't know."

"Two things. First, we're learning more and more about what is called neurocriminology. Through new tests like brain-image scanning, doctors and researchers have found that some individuals are indeed predisposed to violence. It can be genetic."

Agent White nodded. "What's the saying: 'three generations of imbeciles are enough'?"

"Something like that," the profiler responded. "Neurocriminology focuses on physical deformities, functional abnormalities, and certain genes that can make people more prone to violence. It really has nothing to do with lower IQ.

"Which leads me into the second thing," Caleb continued. "Anti-social personality disorders. Many serial killers often exhibit these traits."

"Like a psychopath?" asked Reagan.

"Psychopath or sociopath. Given this guy's ability to go undetected for so long, if the FEB Killer is one of the two, chances are he's a sociopath. A psychopath's actions are usually more erratic, and they have very little impulse control. A psychopath is also more likely to leave behind clues. A sociopath, on the other hand, typically exhibits very controlled behavior. Risks are more calculated and their criminal schemes are more elaborate."

"That sounds like our guy," Allen said.

"Maybe," countered Reagan. "Keep in mind we still don't know if it's just one person behind all of this. Remember they only started calling it the FEB Killer when we asked them to drop the terrorist label."

Allen nodded. "Alright, true. Thanks for the info," he said to Caleb the profiler. "Time for us to get back up to the twelfth floor."

****

The next morning, while Allen was on the phone with police in Charleston, West Virginia, Reagan quietly left the conference room and walked down the hall to her boss' office. She tapped on the door frame to get his attention. "Sir?" she asked. "Can I speak with you for a minute?"

Without looking away from his computer screen, Molina replied: "Yeah, sure. Come on in. Just give me a second to finish sending this email."

Agent White closed the door behind her before sitting down in a chair directly opposite her boss. He looked up after he finished typing, but Reagan continued to sit in silence.

When she still didn't say anything after a few minutes, Molina finally said: "I don't have all day, White. Either talk or leave." The Assistant Deputy Director leaned back in his chair and rested his hands behind his head. Molina could tell that something was bothering his star agent - she was never nervous around him - but he was also swamped with work and didn't have time to sit around waiting on her to finally speak.

Reagan glanced over her shoulder as if to make sure no one was there. "I –", she began, then stopped and sighed. The usually confident FBI agent looked down at her hands and started fiddling with her watch.

"Agent White . . ."

"Well, sir," Reagan said, "it's a rather sensitive matter." *Shit*, Molina thought. *This is going to be about her and Williams. I told that boy to leave her alone.* Playing dumb, he replied: "I don't want to hear about your personal problems. I'm not a therapist. Or a priest."

"Oh, no. It's nothing like that."

Phew. "Alright then, spit it out," Molina ordered. "I've got stuff to do today."

Reagan closed her eyes and took a deep breath. She then slid forward in her chair. By this point, on account of her unusual behavior, Agent White had her boss' full attention.

"I'm just going to come right out and say it. There's no easy way." Reagan breathed deeply again, exhaling in an audible huff. "I think Agent Williams might be our target."

The color drained from Bruce Molina's face and he slowly lowered his arms from behind his head. He then rubbed his face up and down with his hands, trying to wrap his brain around what his best field agent had just told him. ADD Molina had been working with Agent White long enough to know that she wouldn't have brought this to him unless she had some pretty concrete proof.

"Alright. Let's hear it. Why."

"It just all adds up in a way that makes sense," Reagan replied, fidgeting in her chair. "Think about the profile we've been given for the suspect: white, male, single, young. Smart, with training in science or tactical warfare." Reagan knew she was rambling now but couldn't seem to stop it. "Think about it: what does Allen do for the FBI? Before this case, it was his job to travel around the country and come up with ways that terrorists might attack us. It was his job to know our weak points. He's done extensive research on weapons of mass destruction and how they might be introduced into the public, and he's an agent so he knows exactly which tactics we would use to try to solve the case. Plus," Reagan paused, "have you ever been to his apartment? Seen the car he drives? He's sitting on a lot of money - way more than an FBI agent would make. I know his parents are wealthy, but his dad made a show of saying that Allen was on his own financially."

"The money thing is interesting," her boss replied, "but this is all still conjecture, White. I need proof. Not to mention: he's been with you the whole time except for the first drop. There's no way he could've done the second and third weekends."

"I know. I know," Reagan replied, holding up her hands. "He would have to be working with someone, obviously. And I know I don't have any hard evidence. Trust me: I hope it's not him. I'm just saying it might be worth it to have somebody check him out. Run his financials to see where the money is coming from. Come on, sir, we keep saying that everyone is a suspect, but then we immediately rule out anyone who carries a badge for the Bureau."

As much as he didn't want to admit it, Reagan's boss knew that she had a point. And Allen Williams did fit the profile perfectly. "Alright," Molina said, "here's what I'll do. If Williams is the guy - and that's a huge if - if he's the guy, then we wouldn't want him to know he was a suspect. And gossip travels fast in this building . . . it's like you people are just a bunch of oversized middle schoolers with guns."

Reagan couldn't help but laugh. "Yes sir, I agree. But I can't really investigate him while we're working the case together."

"No, you're right. You can't. But I can. You keep doing what you've been doing: following leads, examining evidence; act like nothing has changed. In the meantime, I'll do a bit of digging on Williams' past and see if I can get a sealed warrant to search his apartment. Shouldn't be too difficult given the gravity of the situation."

"Okay," Reagan said, standing up from her chair. "Sounds like a plan."

Before Agent White could get to the door, Molina added: "be careful, White. Don't act any differently around him."

"Yes sir."

FORTY-THREE

Later that day, while Allen researched suspects and Reagan tried to act normal around her partner, Bruce Molina was huddled up in his office examining confidential internal affairs documents about one of the Bureau's best agents. *This is insane*, the Assistant Deputy Director thought as he flipped through page after page of performance reviews wherein Agent Williams received highest marks. *There's no way he could be our guy.* A second later, though, Molina knew he was wrong. Allen Williams could be their guy. Everything Reagan had said made sense. The background in terrorism strategies. The extra money Allen always seemed to have.

Bruce shook his head as the pendulum swung back in favor of denial. *It's too complicated a scheme to do by himself. And he's been around all this time . . . no . . . it's not possible. We would've picked up some kind of communication about it. There's no way.*

Across town, the same back-and-forth 'he did it/there's no way' was running through Reagan's mind. Wanting to get some time away from her partner so she could do a more thorough investigation on him, Agent White had suggested that the two work from their respective homes that evening. "Get out of this stuffy conference room and to a more comfortable environment."

Allen took the bait, not suspecting a thing, and Reagan now found herself alone in her apartment, the silence she once loved now seeming strange after four weeks working with Agent Williams.

Reagan changed out of her work clothes and into sweatpants and a UCF t-shirt before plopping herself down on the couch next to her cat. "Have you missed me, big guy?" she asked as the large Persian ran himself up and down her arm. "Yeah, I know you have. I'm sorry. This case has just been crazy."

The cat purred his response and curled up in a ball next to his owner. Reagan gave Ari a quick pat on the head and then opened her laptop on the coffee table in front of her. "Okay, Aristotle," she said, "let's find out what Agent Williams has been up to recently."

In order to prevent Allen from finding out what she was doing, Reagan used her personal computer to log into the FBI's information database. She saw essentially the same reports that her boss did . . . all signs pointing to Allen Williams as Boy Scout of the Year. *But what about the money?* she thought. *His family is rich, but his dad said he didn't give Allen any money.*

Agent White's next search, after the personnel file, was bank records. Immediately, something in Allen's checking account caught her attention. "Twenty-five hundred dollars a month, every month, from someone called CMI." Reagan scrunched her eyebrows together in confusion. "What in the world is that, Ari?"

****

On the other side of the Virginia-Maryland divide, the man who Molina and White should have been investigating worked late and then enjoyed a nice pasta dinner alone. Joseph passed the time after dinner and before bed by watching the news, gleefully soaking in reports about how the FBI still didn't have any solid leads regarding who the FEB Killer might be.

In between FBI Headquarters and Dr. Carlson's North Bethesda home, in a quaint neighborhood just north of Silver Spring, Joseph's assistant Keri Dupree had just returned to her living room after putting her young son to sleep for the night. Keri's husband, Scott, muted the TV when she walked in. "Okay, Dr. Dupree," he said. "You're going to have to help me on this one."

"On what one?"

"This flesh-eating virus," Scott said, pointing the remote at the television. When Keri looked, she saw that it was a news special about the ongoing outbreaks. "I don't get it," her husband continued. "They're saying it's deliberate, but how does somebody intentionally put a flesh-eating virus into the water? I mean don't we test our drinking water for all of that stuff?"

"Well . . ." Keri began.

"And why the hell aren't you working on this case?" Scott interrupted. "Shouldn't Carlson have another task force going?"

Keri smiled at her trial lawyer husband. She knew Scott wasn't meaning to interrogate her, but when he got on a roll the questions came out of his mouth like a Gatlin-gun running full speed. "Can I answer the questions now, counselor?"

"Oh, yeah. Sorry."

"Not a problem," Keri replied, patting him on the knee as she sat down on the couch. "I'll go in reverse order. We aren't working on this case because it's completely different from a medical standpoint. The tainted blood outbreaks presented two problems: we didn't know what it was and, once we did, it was a virus. There was no way to cure the patients who got the disease. Our work was all about figuring out exactly how the patients were getting sick and then creating a test to screen for the virus and prevent people from getting it in the first place."

"And this time around?"

"The water is infected with a bacteria," answered Keri. "It's treatable. Well, this particular bacteria has a very strong resistance to antibiotics, but from a medical standpoint we know what the problem is and we know, in theory, how to treat it."

"Think about it," Dr. Dupree continued. "Even the way the events are being framed on TV is different. The emphasis on the task force was the virus - the villain was inanimate: it was 'SuperAIDS.' With the current outbreaks the focus is on a person. The FEB Killer. This is much more of a police mystery than a medical one."

"I guess that makes sense," Scott said. "But how is it even possible? We clean all of our water in big treatment plants. And they said on the news that all of those places have extra security now to make sure nobody is breaking into them."

Keri nodded. "We do. I agree," she shrugged, "it doesn't make much sense. It's easy to see why the police are having such a hard time finding whoever is behind it." Keri paused. "Then again, the list of possible suspects can't be all that long. I mean, first the person - or people - would have to find or create a bacteria that is capable of getting past all of the cleaning procedures at the water treatment plants. That is definitely no easy task. When you think about it, all of the new outbreaks are occurring on the weekends, so the FEB Killer probably has a day job. And whoever it is must have some sort of background or special knowledge of police investigation tactics because he's managed to evade the authorities for this long."

Scott nodded. "You're right. There can't be that many people who fit into all of those categories." He took a long pause. "If you take away the police tactics part, though, you do."

"I do what?"

"Fit the categories," he said. Seeing the anger rising on his wife's face, he laughed and quickly added: "not that I think you would ever do something like that. I'm just saying you're smart enough to."

Keri rolled her eyes. "Thanks . . . I think."

A crying baby interrupted their conversation.

"I've got him," Scott said, rising from the couch. "You stay here and keep thinking about your next killer virus."

He then darted out of the room, narrowly avoiding being hit by the pillow that Keri threw at his head.

****

The next morning, Keri was still thinking about her conversation with her husband the night before. Deep in thought, Dr. Dupree jumped when there was a knock on the door.

"Skoos me, Dr. Dupree?"

"Umm, yes?" Keri recognized the man standing in her office doorway as the building's custodian, but she had never spoken to him before beyond a friendly 'hi' or 'good night.'

"Can I as you a queshon?"

Keri put down the test tube in her hands and took off the magnifying glasses she was wearing. "Sure," she said. "How can I help you?"

The custodian shifted back and forth on his feet. "Umm, well, I am Marconi. I clean dee office. I am wanting to know if Dr. Carlson is okay?"

"As far as I know. Why do you ask?"

The nervous shifting continued. "Dr. Carlson always talk with me on weekend, but he was no here las weekend."

"He was speaking at a conference in Boston this past weekend," Keri explained.

"Oh. And weekends before that too?"

"No," Keri shook her head. *That's weird. Isaac always works weekends*, she thought. *Maybe I didn't understand him correctly.* "He hasn't been here the past two weekends?" she asked.

"No. Four," the custodian corrected.

Keri's conversation with Scott the night before instantly came back to her mind. *A doctor with the knowledge to create such a bacteria. Probably has a day job since the attacks have been on weekends. Must be super smart to have evaded police for this long.*

Dr. Dupree's brown eyes grew as big as saucers and her face turned ghostly white. *Oh my God.* Tears filled her eyes. *Oh my God.*

"Doctor?" Marconi said. "You okay?"

Keri blinked back tears and nodded her head. "Yeah, yeah. I'm fine. And Dr. Carlson is fine. He's probably just been working out of the lab at his house." Her mind flashed to the Thursday before last, when Isaac knocked on her office door about five o'clock and said he'd be working at his home lab the next day. *Oh my God.*

The Brazilian immigrant in the doorway looked at her skeptically but wasn't going to challenge someone with the rank and reputation of Dr. Dupree. "Okay. I go back to work now."

As soon as her visitor left, Keri got up from her workstation and shut her office door. The tears she had been blinking back overflowed down her face, and a sudden wave of nausea sent her running from her office door to the trash can by her desk. Keri's breakfast oatmeal and coffee soon filled the wastebasket.

"Oh my God. Oh my God oh my God OH MY GOD!"

She struggled to choke back her tears. "It's him. It's Isaac. Oh my God. I'm working for a terrorist. Oh. My. G-"

Keri's words were interrupted by another round of vomiting.

When her stomach finally settled and her tears slowed to a dribble, Dr. Dupree wiped her face and mouth and tried to fix her hair as best she could. Keri then grabbed her purse and her car keys, knowing exactly what she had to do next.

FORTY-FOUR

In Atlanta, Dr. David Malhotra of the Centers for Disease Control was giving a guest lecture at Emory Medical School. The biomedical researcher's cell phone buzzed loudly on the podium in front of him.

"I'm sorry about this," Dr. Malhotra apologized, glancing down to read the text message. "I have a patient in the hospital that I might have to leave here to tend to."

"I thought you didn't treat patients?" a student called out.

"I almost never do. This is an exception - an aid worker from Haiti. The locals claimed that they cursed her with some voodoo disease, and so far we're having a hell of a time treating her symptoms."

A flash of relief crossed David's face when he saw that the text was from his wife and not the hospital. 'Need hamburger meat and rice from store for Gus. He ate Jane's volcano project. Vet said should be fine with few days of bland diet.' The doctor shook his head and sighed at his chocolate lab's latest antics. Gus loved to eat paper, so it shouldn't have been a surprise that he would go after David's daughter's paper mache volcano.

Remembering his audience, the doctor was about to resume his speech when his cell phone buzzed again. "Sorry. Again," David apologized.

The second text also was not from the hospital. It did, however, catch Dr. Malhotra's attention. 'Hey David, it's Keri Dupree. Been a long time. Give me a call when you get a minute, please.'

Dr. Dupree had worked with David on a task force a few years back, but he hadn't spoken with her since just after his son Matty's funeral. *What in the world could she want?* he wondered. Putting his phone in his pocket, Dr. Malhotra knew his curiosity would have to wait. He had a lecture to give.

****

About forty-five minutes later, after his lecture ended and he had looked in on his hospital patient, David decided to head home to check on his dog. Even though it was midday, the commute could easily top thirty minutes in Atlanta traffic. *More than enough time to call Keri*, he thought. David didn't want to make the phone call after he got home; he didn't want his wife to know anything about it. The task force that introduced Keri and David was the same one that failed to save the life of David's young son, and his wife Mary had all but forbidden the mention of anyone or anything related to the SuperAIDS outbreak.

Dr. Malhotra quickly punched the digits for Keri's phone into the keypad on his dashboard. Seconds later, a loud ringing sound filled the car.

"Hello?"

"Keri? It's David Malhotra."

David could almost hear the woman's smile through the line. "David, hi. How are you?"

"I'm fine," he replied, a little too curtly. It was in that moment that David realized his wife wasn't the only one who associated the task force with Matty's death. Adjusting his tone of voice to try to sound friendlier, he added: "you wanted me to call?"

Keri Dupree hadn't really known what to expect when - or rather, if - David called her back. The two hadn't spoken in over two years; the last time was when Keri called him after his son's funeral to offer her condolences. *He could have been a little more friendly, though*, she thought as she made her own brutal drive from the National Institutes of Health in Bethesda into the heart of Washington, DC traffic. Not wanting to wait for David's reply, she was already headed in the direction of the FBI Headquarters to tell them about Dr. Carlson.

Shaking her head to clear out any hurt feelings, Keri responded: "yes, I did want you to call. Thanks so much for getting back to me back so soon." Dr. Dupree paused again, trying to give the previously chatty Dr. Malhotra a chance to say something. When she only heard silence, Keri said: "I have a question for you. It's kind of random and if you don't want to answer it you don't have to. It's about the virus we worked on."

This time David didn't pull any punches with his words or his tone. "I can't imagine why you'd think I wouldn't want to answer a question about the virus that killed my son."

Keri grimaced. "I know, I know. I'm sorry."

"No, you don't know," David interrupted. "And I pray that you never have to know." His hands gripped the steering wheel so tightly that his knuckles started to turn white. "But ask your question anyway."

Keri took a deep breath. "Okay. Here it goes. What if we were wrong about the virus?"

"What do you mean?"

"What if it wasn't a spontaneous mutation?" she asked. "What if somebody created it and then somehow poisoned the blood with it?"

David's interest was piqued now. "Where's this coming from, Keri?"

"I don't know exactly," his former colleague and friend replied. "Something about this new antibiotic-resistant flesh eating bacteria reminds me of our virus. I just have this gut instinct that the two are related."

David bristled at Keri's reference to SuperAIDS being 'their' virus. It wasn't his. He didn't create it. He didn't even figure out how to stop it. Isaac Carlson did that. "So what's your question?" he asked, knowing Keri well enough to know that she still hadn't dropped the hammer.

"If they're both man-made, the virus and the bacteria, then the list of people capable of creating something like that has to be pretty short."

"And you and I are both on it," David added.

"But who else?"

Dr. Malhotra sighed, releasing his steering wheel death grip for long enough to run one hand through his jet black hair. "Gill isn't there yet," David began, referring to his CDC colleague and fellow task force member. "He hasn't been practicing long enough to know everything he'd need to know. Same for Leah Mann."

"Mmm hmm, agreed. And I don't think Anthony Russo would have it in him," Keri commented.

"Me neither." David hit his breaks at yet another red light. "Of doctors in the United States, with the know-how and personality required to do something like that . . . if I had to pick one person, I'd pin it on your boss."

"Isaac."

"Yep."

Dr. Dupree slumped her shoulders and hung her head as much as possible while still driving. "That's what I thought, too."

She heard a note of anger mix into David's next words. "Do you really think it was him? Spending all that time in the lab, pretending to search for a cure to a disease he created?"

"I don't know, David. I honestly don't know. I mean, I know Isaac can be an asshole at times . . . " Keri sighed heavily. "I just don't know. Or maybe I do but I don't want to believe it. It's hard to think that my boss of eleven years could be a terrorist."

"Thanks for talking it through with me, though," Keri added. "I didn't know who else I could ask."

"You're welcome," Dr. Malhotra said. "And Keri?"

"Yeah?"

"Be careful, alright? If Carlson is who you think he is, he's dangerous."

"I will be. Thanks."

FORTY-FIVE

Unaware of Dr. Dupree's activities, Reagan and Allen continued to plug away in their conference room. However, nearly a month into her investigation and with no real progress to show for it, Agent White was frustrated. Very frustrated.

Reagan stood up from her chair in the conference room and began to pace the floor. She ran her hands through her not-quite-red hair and groaned.

"Alright," her partner said in response. "I give. What is it?"

"Nothing."

"No, seriously," Allen said, "what is it?"

"Seriously: nothing. We have nothing. The FEB Killer has been running around for a month now and all we have to show for our investigation is a couple of falsely accused suspects and a map with post-it notes on it." Reagan sighed. "I've got to be missing something. Something doesn't fit."

"Like?" Allen asked.

"I don't know. But something."

Agent White stopped her pacing, went back to her chair, and started packing her notebook and cell phone into her briefcase.

"Where are you going?"

"Bethesda," Reagan answered. "I've been over the files a thousand times and can't come up with anything, so maybe the missing clue isn't police-related. Maybe it has to do with the bacteria itself." She slung her bag over her shoulder and walked toward the conference room door. "I'm going to talk to Isaac Carlson at the NIH. I worked with him a little bit on the SuperAIDS investigation . . . maybe he can give some insight into the flesh-eating bacteria."

****

About forty-five minutes after Reagan's departure, the phone in the middle of the conference table issued a loud beep.

"Agent Williams," the receptionist said via speakerphone, "I have a Dr. Keri Dupree here to see you. She's from the National Institutes of Health."

Allen looked up from the files he was reading and checked the clock. One-fifteen. *I don't remember scheduling anything for today.* Clicking the talk button, Allen said, "does she have an appointment?"

The machine fell silent, then: "she says it's about the FEB Killer and that it's urgent."

Agent Williams knew that any visitors would have their identification checked and go through a metal detector, so he wasn't worried about security. *This better be good,* he thought. *Time is not something I have any extra of. Especially with Reagan out on a wild goose chase.*

A few minutes later, a well-dressed, attractive woman in her late thirties knocked on Allen's door. "Excuse me, Agent Williams?"

"Are you Dr. Dupree?"

The woman nodded.

"Come on in," Allen said, standing up to shake his visitor's hand and close the conference room door behind her. Sitting back down at the table, he said: "what can I do for you?"

Keri wasted no time. "It's actually what I can do for you. Like I told the front desk, I work at the NIH in Bethesda. I'm the Deputy Chief of Pathology."

"Yeah, about that. You work with Isaac Carlson, right?"

A flash of something Allen couldn't quite register crossed Dr. Dupree's face.

"I do," she answered. "He's my boss."

Allen nodded. "That's right. Yeah, you really didn't have to trek all the way in here with whatever information

you have. My partner, Reagan White, is headed out to
Bethesda right now to meet with Carlson."

The flash came back to Keri's face, but this time it
stayed. And Agent Williams recognized it: fear.

"She's meeting with Isaac? Right now?"

Allen didn't like the tone in his visitor's voice. "You
better start talking, Dr. Dupree. And fast."

"I think it's him," Keri blurted out. "I think - I think he's
the one poisoning the water."

Under less pressing circumstances, Allen would've
noted the absurdity of the assertion. Isaac Carlson was a
national treasure. President Hughes had said so himself. The
man was a medical genius . . . it was his job to save lives, not
take them.

But with the Deputy Chief of Pathology sitting in front
of him saying her boss was a terrorist, and with Reagan in the
same room with said potential terrorist, now was not the time
for Allen to play armchair psychologist.

"Tell me why," he demanded.

Keri had her arguments ready to go. "First, and I know
this because I'm a member of this group, there are very few
people in the world capable of making this kind of
sophisticated bacteria. He's one of them."

"Next."

"He's been out-of-town every weekend since the
outbreaks started. Isaac always, and I mean always, works on
the weekends. At least every Saturday and a lot of Sundays. I
talked with the janitor and checked with security in our
building and Isaac hasn't come in to the office any weekends
this past month."

"Anything else?" The story was sounding plausible to
Allen, but he wanted more information.

"He's not worried about the water."

"What do you mean?"

Keri took a deep breath. "He's the only person I know
who isn't drinking filtered or bottled water. He's not even

worried about it. I mean, he's a doctor. He knows exactly how horrible of a disease this is, but . . . " Keri paused to look for the right words.

Allen found them for her. "He knows he's safe because he didn't poison any of the water around here," he said.

"Exactly," Keri nodded.

Panic punched Allen in the gut and he immediately grabbed the phone on his desk to dial Reagan's number. When she didn't answer, he picked up his cell phone and, heart racing and fingers shaking, managed to type a text message:

'Get out now. It's Carlson. IT'S CARLSON!!!!'

FORTY-SIX

Reagan saw her phone light up that she had an incoming call. Not wanting to be rude, she ignored it. A few seconds later the phone buzzed with a text message alert.

"Sorry," she apologized to the doctor seated in front of her. "I need to check this really quickly."

At first the words that Allen frantically typed didn't seem real. *What does he mean: it's Carlson? No it's not.* A split second later though, and perhaps a consequence of the all-caps screaming at the end of the text message, Reagan knew her partner wouldn't lie to her. *Shit. I walked straight into the lion's den.*

All of Reagan's FBI training told her to play it cool. To not, under any circumstances, let the suspect in front of her know that he had been made. So she smiled, calmly put her cell phone back in her briefcase, and apologized again for checking it. Agent White then asked a few more generic questions about bacterial outbreaks and historical responses to them. It didn't matter anymore; Reagan had her man. Dr. Joseph Isaac Carlson, Jr., the middle-aged genius sitting across the desk from her, was also the mass murderer she had been looking for. Reagan had literally come face to face with evil. With the domestic terrorist whose bacterial attacks gripped the nation in fear. *Stay calm*, Reagan reminded herself. *You have no backup. He clearly has no reservations about killing people. Stay calm, and then get out.*

When the opportunity presented itself, Reagan did just that. Rising from her chair, she smiled again and forced herself to shake hands with the madman. "Thank you so much for meeting with me. Again."

The middle-aged doctor returned her smile, but Reagan couldn't help but notice that the smile didn't quite reach his stormy blue eyes. "It was my pleasure," he said. "Hopefully if we meet again it will be under different circumstances."

Agent White wasn't fooled for a second by Dr. Carlson's charm, but she could easily see how others would be. *I was the first time around*, she admitted. *Heck, I was until ten minutes ago.* J. Isaac Carlson was smart, well-spoken, confident, and not altogether unfortunate looking. *Just like Ted Bundy*, Reagan mused.

Nodding her head and stooping down to pick up her briefcase, Agent White agreed with Isaac's comment. "Yes, hopefully very different circumstances."

"Can you find your way out or shall I show you the way?"

It took all of Reagan's mental strength to not betray the fear that washed over her. *Under absolutely no circumstances do I want to be around him any longer than necessary.* Taking a deep breath to compose herself, she answered: "no, I think I remember how to go. Elevators are down the hall and to the right, and then turn left when I get off on the first floor."

"Yep, you've got it. Have a good day, Agent White."

"Uh . . . y-you too."

Reagan was caught off-guard by Dr. Carlson's well wishes. *He really is a sick bastard*, she thought as she turned right out of his office and walked toward the elevators at the end of the hall. *A sick, sick bastard. But we got him.* The light that had been missing from her eyes ever since she read Allen's text now returned. *He won't hurt anyone anymore. We got him.*

****

Joseph knew the exact moment when Reagan White found out that he was responsible for the biological attacks. She tried to hide it, and did a fairly good job, but not good enough.

He saw the flash of confusion, followed quickly by fear, as she read the text message on her phone. And he saw it in her eyes when she looked back up at him. Two blue-green pools of panic. *Much to Agent White's credit*, thought Joseph, *her voice wasn't noticeably different. Although I did catch her off guard by wishing her well at the end of our conversation.* He chuckled. *Stupid woman.*

Joseph's happy mood didn't last long, though. He knew he had to hurry. Grabbing his car keys from the side pocket of his briefcase, Joseph ran over to his office door and looked around the corner, just in time to catch a glimpse of Agent White as she turned to walk down the hall housing the elevators.

Whereas Reagan had gone right, Joseph went left, bolting down the hall at a full sprint and crashing through the door that led to the stairwell. Taking the concrete steps two at a time, Joseph quickly reached the first floor of his office building. He then continued his mad dash, going out the side exit and making a beeline for his car.

Joseph was breathing heavily by the time he sat down in the driver's seat and cranked up his trusty silver sedan. "Fuck," he exclaimed in between breaths, "I'm out of shape."

It was in that moment that Joseph saw the object of his attention exiting the front doors of the National Institutes of Health. Shifting his car into gear, Joseph's tires squealed as he slammed his foot down on the gas pedal and took off. Directly in his sights was Agent Reagan White.

****

Reagan's mind was admittedly elsewhere when she left the front doors of the NIH building and started walking to her car. She pulled her briefcase around in front of her and started digging to find her phone to call Allen. Now that the FBI had a solid suspect, they would need to get a warrant to search his house. *We should probably also go ahead and arrest - "*

Agent White didn't have time to finish her thought. Joseph's car prevented that from happening. The front end of the car, to be exact. Dr. Carlson's sedan had already reached a speed in excess of fifty miles per hour when he crashed it into the side of the unsuspecting FBI agent.

Reagan heard and felt the bones in her right leg snap. Her next sensation was one of flying, as her long, lean body bounced up and over the windshield and roof of the car before careening back down onto the hard, black asphalt. After that, all Reagan felt was pain.

FORTY-SEVEN

"Shit. Shit shit shit!"

Joseph screamed at his windshield, pounding his hands on the steering wheel in time with each tinge of profanity.

"I'm fucked now."

The doctor couldn't figure out where he had gone wrong. Driving well above the speed limit and pausing at red lights only long enough to make sure the intersection was clear, Joseph drove like the madman that he was, knowing that his only chance to make it out now was to destroy every piece of evidence that could possibly tie him to the SuperAIDS and FEB outbreaks.

"But how the hell did they figure it out?" Dr. Carlson knew he was racing against the clock, knew he should instead be thinking about how to get rid of everything in his secret lab before the FBI busted down his door. *If they haven't already*, he thought. "Fuck!"

This time Joseph's expletive came half from frustration at the situation and half in response to his having to swerve to narrowly miss the woman in his neighborhood who was out walking her dogs. "I should've just run her over," he mumbled. "Wouldn't make any difference now."

And that was when it hit him. The missing link. The thing he had forgotten. The doctor's car may have been screeching into his driveway practically on two wheels, but in that moment his mind was perfectly clear.

An escape plan.

Joseph shoved the car's gear into park and yanked his keys out of the ignition, running as fast as his legs would carry him to his front door. So far, much to his relief, he still didn't see any police cars.

"You didn't plan an escape. What kind of fucking idiot doesn't plan his own escape?"

The public persona of Isaac was lecturing the private Joseph now as the man threw his front door shut behind him. He made it halfway to his kitchen before remembering the lock.

"And we all know what happened the last time you didn't lock the door," he said. "Peyton happened."

Peyton Finch, the elementary school-aged Girl Scout who went to her neighbor's house to try to sell some cookies but ended up dead and buried in the national park.

Quickly returning to the front of his house, Joseph locked both the dead bolt and the door handle. He then spun back around on the hardwood floors and ran to his kitchen.

The code to open the door of Dr. Carlson's secret underground lab wasn't particularly hard to figure out - it was the date he graduated from medical school. Joseph punched in the six-digit code, listening for the hiss-pop sound that would let him know the door was unlocked.

All the while, America's most wanted terrorist continued to berate himself. Ducking his head and stepping down into his lair, careful to shut and lock the hidden door behind him, Joseph rambled on:

"You did everything else right. The virus was untraceable. Untreatable. Hell, everyone on my task force was convinced that it was just a spontaneous mutation."

The doctor reached the floor of his lab, grabbed a hammer out of a drawer, and began smashing flash drives containing years' worth of facts and figures. The cracking sound of shattered electronics accentuated Joseph's ranting.

"Sure," he said with another swing of the hammer, "they found Peyton's body in the woods. But they never found the blood donors. And nobody questioned me about any of it. All four murders are still listed as unsolved."

More broken plastic littered the floor.

When Carlson finished with the small rectangular USB drives that stored his priceless research, he turned his attention and his hammer toward his computers, smashing them into thousands of shiny little pieces. Then, for good measure, he filled a bucket of water and poured it over all of the debris, intent on ensuring that no electronic evidence would be found.

****

While Joseph was busy obliterating his lab, Allen Williams focused all of his resources on investigating Dr. Carlson. Computers were hacked, bank and phone records examined, and a secure call placed to a federal judge for a warrant to search the doctor's house. For every one call Allen made to an FBI or Joint Terrorism Task Force official, he made another one to Reagan's cell phone. *Why the hell isn't she answering?*

Fifteen minutes later, Allen found himself in the back seat of a FBI sedan, part of a caravan of official black vehicles traveling at breakneck pace from Washington, DC to Dr. Carlson's North Bethesda home.

Agent Williams' legs and hands were shaking. They had their man. Allen was nervous to be part of his first big bust, but he was also angry. Really angry. A few minutes earlier his cell phone had rung, and his boss was on the other end. Bruce Molina had finally located Reagan. She was in the hospital in critical condition after being run over in the NIH parking lot, and all signs pointed to it being Carlson's car. *We've gotta nail this sonofabitch. He's going down.*

Allen's phone rang again. "Agent Williams."

"Williams, this is Kehoe from IT."

Allen could barely hear anything over the wail of sirens from the line of police cars. "It's too loud," he yelled into the receiver. "I can't hear you. Email me what you found."

A minute later his phone dinged with a new message.

To: Williams, Allen

From: Kehoe, Jack
Re: Carlson records

Phone calls and text messages didn't show anything suspicious. His home wireless provider gave us the past six months of his internet history - also nothing suspicious. A broader search of his public activities showed him swiping an access card to Maryland university libraries numerous times six-to-nine months ago. Hit the jackpot with his internet search card at the library. Carlson did multiple engine searches for addresses and facility designs of affected water treatment plants. Probably the only information he couldn't find out without internet help. Also, his satellite radio company was able to ping his car's travel history for us. Places suspect's car in each outbreak location when they happened. And a heads up: Carlson is registered in Maryland as owning a 9mm Beretta and a suppressor.

Allen typed a quick "thanks" in reply. On a hunch, he added: "run a search for me please. All unsolved murders in DC area in past five years. Only the weird ones, though."

Turning to the agent driving the car, Allen said: "It's him. No doubts now."

FORTY-EIGHT

Joseph's first indication that the cavalry had arrived was the crash. Wood cracking, hinges breaking, and what sounded like dozens of footsteps above his head.

"Shit. They're here," Joseph said, his hands fumbling nervously as he flipped on an intercom system that allowed him to hear what was happening upstairs. He then rushed to the other end of the room, pulling his small, white test mice out of their cages and tossing them into a large metal trash can. Adding to the pile the few documents he had printed off and stored in his workstation, Joseph lit a match and set the papers and the little animals on fire.

"We know you're here, Carlson," a male voice boomed from upstairs. "Come out now. Surrender and this will be easier on all of us."

The owner of the home ignored the instructions of his uninvited guests. Joseph knew he still had some time. The police didn't know about his underground lab . . . yet. Which was good. Joseph needed more time. He still had dozens of vials of bacteria left to destroy.

Upstairs, Allen and his SWAT team searched what looked like an empty house for any clues that a terrorist lived there. All they found was a well-appointed home with a minimalist decoration scheme. No sign of the doctor or his evil machinations.

Standing in the front foyer, Allen called out: "I know you're in here, Carlson. Your car is in the driveway. And I know you can hear me. So come on out. I just want to talk."

Just wants to talk. Bullshit, Joseph thought downstairs.

Agent Williams slowly walked from the front of the house to the back, talking loudly the whole time.

"The funny thing is, Carlson, if you hadn't run over my partner in the NIH parking lot, I might not have been able to get probable cause for a search warrant yet. Or at least wouldn't have gotten the warrant as quickly as I did. But your office building has security cameras," Allen continued. "Did you know that? We've got you and your silver sedan on tape running over Agent White. And guess what that means, doctor? That means this is now an active manhunt. You tried to murder an FBI agent. I can search wherever I damn well please until I find your sorry ass."

****

Outside of Dr. Carlson's home, the news media descended in droves. First on the scene was Channel Seven News.

"This is Marissa Zimmermann, reporting live from North Bethesda, Maryland where the FBI and local police have a residential street completely blocked off. Officials are being very tight-lipped at the moment, but I have learned that federal investigators believe they have found the person or people responsible for the flesh-eating bacteria outbreaks. I cannot overstate the number of police officials on the scene. Dozens and dozens of vehicles and law enforcement officers. I'm told that FBI SWAT is in charge right now, and it appears that they are focusing on one house in particular.

"Like I said, this is a developing story and we are being given very little information, but to repeat: federal officials have surrounded a house here in the northern suburbs of Washington, DC and are believed to be hunting for the FEB Killer. I will be here, trying to get more information to report, until this situation is resolved. Back to you in the studio, Phillip."

Twenty minutes later, one reporter and some bystanders had turned into thirty reporters and a massive crowd that required extra police just to control it. Remaining on the scene and reporting live was the veteran newscaster from Channel Seven.

"Marissa Zimmermann again, still reporting to you live from Crabapple Street in North Bethesda, where it appears that the FBI has entered into some sort of siege situation in the house of the man believed to be the FEB Killer. We have now learned more about the home involved. Authorities will not say how many people are in the house or if it belongs to the suspected terrorist. What I can tell you is that the home in question is owned by Dr. J. Isaac Carlson, the Chief of Pathology at the National Institutes of Health in nearby Bethesda. A very surprising development is that this is also the same street where a little girl went missing nearly two years ago. Eight year old Peyton Finch was playing with other children in the neighborhood when she disappeared, and her body was found buried in Blue Mountain National Park several months later.

"Of course, there is rampant speculation among media and bystanders here, but based on official reports, we've been given no reason to believe that the two events are connected in any way."

"Now I'm not allowed to show you the house under siege in case the suspect is watching television, but we will certainly continue looking for answers in this still-developing story. For now, I'm Marissa Zimmermann, Channel Seven News."

****

Across town at the White House, Daniel Bader hung up his office phone and rose from the chair behind his desk. *He is not going to be happy about this one.* Putting on his suit jacket, the Chief of Staff then crossed the room and entered the adjoining Oval Office.

"Excuse me, Mr. President?"

Richard Hughes looked up from his desk. "You've got bad news."

"I'm sorry, sir?"

"You've got bad news," the president repeated. "That's your bad news voice."

President Hughes' best friend since college grimaced. "You know me too well, sir."

"I do," Hughes nodded. "That's how I also know you're stalling right now. Spit it out."

"We figured out who the FEB Killer is."

The president's eyes lit up. A smile began to spread across his face. "That's fantastic! Why would you think that's bad news?"

The Chief of Staff's eyes and face did not share his boss' joy. "It's Isaac Carlson, Mr. President."

"What does he have to do with anything? He figured out who the killer is?"

"No sir," Bader replied. "He is the killer."

All previous happiness drained from the president's face and was replaced by shock.

"What?"

It was less of a question and more a statement of disbelief.

The deputy nodded his head in confirmation. "Carlson's lab assistant figured it out. Keri Dupree. She went to the FBI Headquarters and turned him in."

"But . . . he . . . he sat right there," Hughes said, pointing to the couch where he and his Chief of Staff once met with Dr. Carlson of the NIH and Dr. Malhotra of the CDC to discuss the SuperAIDS virus.

"Wait," the president said. The light bulb had just gone off in his head. "Was he behind SuperAIDS too?"

The thought hadn't occurred to Daniel Bader. "I don't know, sir."

President Hughes shook his head, still unable to comprehend what his Chief of Staff was saying. "I gave him an award. Shook his hand, looked him in the eye, and thanked him for all of the lives he saved. I thanked him for his service to his country."

"I know, sir. So did I."

Hughes grew serious. "Do they have him?"

"Beg your pardon?"

"Does the FBI have him in custody?"

Daniel shook his head. "Not yet. But they know he's in his house and they have the place surrounded."

"Holy hell," said Hughes with a sigh, running his hand through his gray hair. "Okay. Keep me updated."

FORTY-NINE

Back inside the Carlson home, Allen Williams and his fellow agents were getting frustrated. *There's no way he just disappeared. And the neighbors said he got here not long before we did. Unless he fled on foot?* Allen shook his head. *That wouldn't make any sense. He wouldn't come back here just to drop off his car. He would've gone straight to the interstate and gotten as far away from here as possible.*

While the SWAT team examined the house with a fine-toothed comb, Allen continued trying to coax the suspect out of hiding.

"So I got an email from one of our IT people," he began. "He told me that you've been looking up some interesting things on the internet at the University of Maryland's library. Like where water treatment facilities are located and how they're set up. I don't know . . . that seems like a pretty funny thing to be researching. Unless you were going to attack them." Allen continued to talk as he paced through the first floor of the house. "My friend in IT also said that you like to listen to satellite radio. I don't have satellite radio - the regular version is good enough for me. But that satellite stuff is cool," he commented. "Did you know that the radio company can pinpoint your car's location based on which satellite your radio is pinging? It works just like a GPS. We know everywhere your car has been ever since you signed up for the subscription."

Downstairs, Joseph froze. "Shit!" *I didn't bring my phone on the trips because I knew they could track that, but my radio?* "Fuck!" *They'll get me for all of it now. Including the homeless people and the little brat.*

Agent Williams kept talking upstairs.

"Have you ever heard the story of Jekyll and Hyde?" he asked. "I had to read it in high school, and it always fascinated me. How someone could do such terrible things and then go undetected in regular society. 'The Strange Case of Dr. Jekyll and Mr. Hyde' is the full title. Have you ever read it, Mitchell?" he asked, talking to a SWAT team member beside him.

"No sir, I haven't."

"Like I said," Allen continued, "it's fascinating. You want to hear the story, Carlson? I think you'd like it. I think, in fact I know, that you can identify with it. You see, back in the day there was this law enforcement guy in London. He started investigating a dude named Mr. Hyde because Hyde was beating up random people. Hyde even killed a guy. At the same time, there was a man named Dr. Jekyll who was a fine upstanding citizen. One time, Dr. Jekyll paid restitution to one of Mr. Hyde's victims.

"Do you know how the story ends?" Allen asked, his loud comments carrying throughout the house. "I bet you do. It turns out that Dr. Jekyll and Mr. Hyde are the same person. How about that? A doctor, revered by those who know him, is also an evil murderer."

A hiss-pop sound coming from the island in the middle of the kitchen made everyone in the room jump. The FBI agents and SWAT team members immediately trained their weapons on the island. They then watched in surprise as one end of the counter slowly raised up, revealing a secret stairway.

Before the heavily armed men could begin yelling at their suspect, Joseph spoke. A booming voice coming up at them from below - eerie in its calmness.

"I do like 'Jekyll and Hyde,'" Joseph began, slowly beginning to climb the stairs out of his secret lab. It was difficult, though, given that the stairs were steep and the terrorist doctor could only use one hand on a rail to help himself climb. The other hand was occupied by holding a fully-loaded 9mm handgun to his head.

"It's a great story," Dr. Carlson continued. "The people never see it coming," he added, an arrogant smile spreading over his face.

The SWAT team, along with Agent Williams, backed away from the island as their suspect ascended the stairs, not wanting him to pull the trigger but at the same time more than ready to pull their own.

The blue-gray eyes that had shined so brightly when enticing the homeless Army veteran, Willie 'Shoes' McRae, and Hillary into his car, and the same hypnotic drawl of his voice that convinced Peyton Finch, James Leavey, and Reagan White that Dr. Carlson could be trusted, were now working their magic on Agent Williams and his men.

"The difference between that story and mine," Joseph Carlson, Jr. added, "is that Dr. Jekyll was schizophrenic. I don't have dissociative identity disorder," he explained. The evil smile spread wider. "I'm just a sociopath."

"There is one big similarity between Dr. Jekyll and Dr. Carlson, though," he said, clicking the safety off his gun. "They both kill themselves."

****

The trigger was pulled and the damage done before Allen could do anything to stop it. Now lying in front of him on the kitchen's hardwood floors was the body and splattered brains of one of the world's most brilliant medical minds.

The line between genius and insanity is very thin, Allen thought. He carefully stepped around Joseph's lifeless body and over the growing pool of blood in order to get to the kitchen island. Gun still drawn, unaware of what might await him below, Agent Williams descended into the secret room where Dr. Carlson planned one of the worst acts of domestic terrorism in recent history.

What Allen saw when he reached the bottom, though, shocked him. The concrete room was a destruction zone.

Shattered computer parts lay all over the floor and desks, there were several trash cans full of the ashes of burned documents, and the entire dungeon reeked of a combination of charred animal flesh and bleach.

This is what he was doing the whole time I was upstairs talking, Allen thought. *He was destroying evidence.* The agent shook his head in frustrated disbelief, angry at himself for letting Carlson remove any trace of his illegal actions. *Sure, we know it was him,* Williams thought. *He wouldn't have killed himself if he didn't do it.* "But we can't prove it now." Allen put his gun back in its holster and ran his fingers through his hair. "We can't learn from it either, at least not with regard to future biological weapons."

"Shit!" he yelled, slamming his hand against the wall.

"What?" asked Russ Mitchell, the SWAT team member who had joined him in the basement.

"He got rid of all of the evidence," Allen answered, gesturing around the room. "The computers are shattered. The papers are burned. The lab rats are barbequed. And I'm guessing that bleach smell is from him flushing all of his test chemicals down the sink."

"Yeah," Agent Mitchell said. "But his brain is shattered too. He's dead. It's over."

Allen sighed. "I know. But I still can't shake the feeling that the son of a bitch got away with it."

Agent Williams continued to walk around the no-longer-secret laboratory, trying to tip-toe around the bits and pieces of electronics.

"He's been right here under our noses the whole time. I can't believe it. We all assumed that it was either foreign terrorists at work or some nut job in a cabin in the woods. But here he was: in broad daylight. And Keri Dupree was right . . . out of all of the people in the United States who were capable of making the bacteria from scratch, Carlson obviously tops the list."

Russ Mitchell nodded his head. "Except we would've asked him to help us make the list, giving him the perfect opportunity to sabotage the search."

Allen sighed. "You're probably right."

Footsteps on the stairs caused both men to turn around, just in time to see the Assistant Deputy Director joining them in the safe room.

"He is right," Bruce Molina said. "We always assume the enemy isn't one of us. Our first guess is always the foreigner. Or the recent immigrant with ties to foreign groups. In the rare instances when it turns out the bad guy is a boy-next-door natural-born citizen, we immediately start trying to find ways to disown him. The Unabomber was a recluse - a kook," Molina explained. "Timothy McVeigh hated the government and thought it stood for tyranny. Eric Robert Rudolf? Another survivalist and a homophobic white supremacist. Outsiders. Not 'normal.'"

"And then comes Carlson," Allen added. "Brilliant, successful, highly respected in his field. Honored even by those outside of medicine. A *doctor*, for Pete's sake."

His boss nodded. "He's the worst nightmare. You have a bad dream about the outsider and you tell people. You build walls and you keep them out. But you don't tell anybody about this dream. It's too scary."

FIFTY

"It is a very good afternoon on Crabapple Street in North Bethesda, Maryland," Marissa Zimmermann, the brunette reporter, said with a smile. "Officials have now confirmed that the FEB Killer, the man responsible for the outbreaks of flesh-eating bacteria in several U.S. cities, is dead. I repeat: the FEB Killer is now dead.

"I have to say, Phillip, in all of my years in newscasting I have never seen an event quite like this one. As mentioned previously, hundreds of local, state, and federal police swarmed this quiet suburban street in North Bethesda in search of the FEB Killer. We saw officers in full body armor storm into one house, search dogs were deployed, and helicopters have been flying overhead for nearly an hour. After a long period of inaction, a few minutes ago we heard a single gunshot and then a call over the radio saying 'he's dead.' The mood among the officials I've spoken to is one of absolute relief and elation. I'm told there will be a press conference within the next half hour, which we will of course bring to you live here on Channel Seven."

Allen didn't stay for the press conference. There was somewhere much more important he needed to be. Not bothering to try to remove his car from the mass of vehicles blocking Joseph's street, Agent Williams commandeered the police car closest to the exit and set off in the direction of Suburban Hospital in Bethesda. Reagan had been lucky . . . the NIH building was directly across the street from the trauma center.

****

Reagan heard a soft knock on her hospital room door and slowly opened her eyes. Allen opened the door and was now walking over to her bed, holding something behind his back.

"Hi," she managed to croak. It hard enough to just breathe; speaking one word felt like running a marathon.

Allen smiled down at her, and Reagan struggled to return the gesture. The bruises and swelling on her face made smiling nearly impossible.

"I brought you some contraband," her partner said, swinging a plastic bag around from behind his back and pulling out a pint of ice cream. "Chocolate chip cookie dough. Your favorite, right?"

The patient closed her eyes and slowly moved her head up and down in the affirmative.

"How do you feel?" Allen asked, sitting down on the edge of her bed.

Reagan took a breath, as deep as her broken ribs would allow, and said: "like I got run over by a car."

Allen laughed, but not the same deep-belly laugh that his partner had grown to appreciate. This was a concerned laugh. A nervous, worried laugh. "Well, look at it this way," he said, "you're one of very few people who can say you feel like you got run over by a car and actually know what you're talking about."

Reagan groaned. "I'd rather not know."

"I know. I'm sorry." Trying to keep the mood as light as possible, Allen added: "the puke green and purple colors look good on your face, though."

Agent White opened her eyes again. "Liar."

Williams smiled. "No, really. And the red from the fresh cuts and gashes really gives it something extra."

Reagan was in no mood to joke around, but Allen's positive attitude was infectious. "Compulsive liar," she replied with a small grin.

It's now or never, Allen thought to himself. The smile faded from his face and he reached up to brush a loose piece of hair off his partner's forehead. "You've never looked more beautiful."

Instinctively, Reagan blushed and looked away, caught off guard by Allen's statement. When she finally turned her eyes back, Reagan was surprised to find him still looking down at her. Unsure how to respond, Reagan returned to their previous banter. "Pathological liar."

Undeterred, Allen brushed another piece of strawberry blonde hair out of her hazel eyes. "We got him, Reagan. We got Carlson. It's over. He's over. SuperAIDS, FEB, it was all him. And it's all over."

Reagan breathed a sigh of relief. "Finally."

Allen smiled. "Remember when we first met? How Bruce said we'd complement each other well? He was right."

A wave of guilt washed over Reagan's battered body. She closed her heavy eyelids and whispered: "I thought it was you."

It took a minute for the full meaning of Reagan's confession to hit Allen. He felt like a hammer had just landed square on his chest, and the lump in his throat made it difficult to choke out his response.

"Me?" he asked, shocked by her admission. "You thought I was behind it all? You thought I could do that?"

Reagan nodded her head. A tear slowly rolled down her cheek as she opened her eyes. "I'm sorry. I should've known it couldn't be you. You were just always so full of ideas about different ways to attack the United States . . ."

"It's my *job* to think up all of those things!"

Reagan winced. "I know. I just - " she paused. "What's CMI?"

"What?"

"CMI. They make a deposit into your checking account every month. Who is it?"

"You checked my bank accounts?" Allen asked incredulously. "Are you serious?" He stood up from the hospital bed and ran a frustrated hand through his hair. "CMI stands for Coal Mountain Investments. My grandparents - my mom's parents - set up a trust for me when I was born. It matured when I turned twenty-five and now I get monthly interest payments from it." Allen paused. "I don't believe this . . . you thought that was blood money. You seriously thought I was getting paid by some terrorist organization to tell them where to attack. And what else - sabotage the investigation?"

Allen began to pace the room, seething in anger. Finally he whispered through gritted teeth: "I can't believe you thought I could do something like that."

This time when Reagan winced it wasn't because of the pain from her injuries. "I know," she replied. "I know. I'm sorry. It's my fault," she continued, the guilt Reagan felt rising in her voice with every word she spoke. "If I had focused more on real suspects instead of you, I might have discovered that it was Carlson." A disgusted snort escaped Reagan's nose. "I thought I was so smart to have figured out that the killer was there in front of me. And I was right. Yet still so very, very wrong."

Allen knew he should say something, do something, to comfort his partner. He knew he should forgive her for suspecting him, for thinking him capable of such a heinous crime. He knew he should, but at that moment he just couldn't.

Agent Williams had come to the hospital today with every intention of both celebrating Isaac Carlson's demise and telling the feisty redhead in front of him that somehow, improbably, unexpectedly, he had fallen in love with her.

But now? Allen lowered his head to keep from having to make eye contact with Reagan. He knew he had to say something, but it just wouldn't, couldn't, be what he had initially planned.

"There's no way you could've known that it was Carlson," he said, the emotion that had been present in his voice now replaced by an icy distance. "He had us all fooled.

Hell, it took two separate diseases and over four years for his lab assistant to figure it out." Williams paused. *Look her in the eye, dammit.* Once again, this time with conviction, he repeated: "there's no way you could've known."

Taking the room's silence as his cue, Allen walked from the corner of the room over to Agent White's hospital bed. Even though he was still shocked and hurt that Reagan could suspect him of being a terrorist, the FBI agent couldn't stop himself from bending down and placing a soft kiss on her forehead.

"Feel better soon, White."

EPILOGUE

Three women, one standing and two sitting, watched as the cemetery groundskeeper lowered Joseph Isaac Carlson, Jr.'s casket into the ground. There had been no funeral service; no memorial of any kind. Just this: three women in a row, each with her own reason for being there.

Dr. Keri Dupree had arrived first. Using her job title and connections in the Maryland physicians community, Keri pestered and hounded the medical examiner until he finally told her when and where her boss of eleven years would be buried. Keri's husband, Scott, had told her not to go. "I don't understand why you want to have anything else to do with that monster," he said. Keri didn't understand it either. She simply knew she needed to be there. And so she was, dressed in a black shift dress with dark sunglasses to mask the conflict and pain in her eyes.

Dr. Dupree was who she was that day because of Isaac Carlson. She learned nearly everything she knew about pathology from him - knowledge that would help her now run her own research lab as the new Chief of Pathology. Keri met her lawyer husband while attending a medical conference that Isaac was supposed to go to but had sent her instead. She owed her career, her marriage, her life as she knew it to the man in the simple wooden casket a few feet in front of her. People called him a madman. A terrorist. Keri knew he was those things - after all, she was the one who turned him in - but she also knew a different side. And so she came to pay her last respects to Dr. Carlson, even though the world told her that he didn't deserve them.

The elderly woman seated in a wheelchair beside where Keri stood wasn't much concerned about what the world thought, either. June Carlson was nearing her ninety-seventh birthday, and she came to her grandson's burial because she knew no one else in the family would. She also came because she was certain that her late husband would've wanted her there. Family meant the world to Bo Carlson, and he never could understand how his son turned into such a cold hearted man who neglected his child like he did. June never understood it either. She raised her boy to be kind, caring; to value family as the set of people one could always count on in the world. But little Joey, who grew up to be Joseph Sr., never listened. Never learned. And Joseph Jr. was the result.

A steady stream of tears flowed down through the wrinkles in the woman's face. June was two years old when her father returned from World War I, lived through the Great Depression, World War II, and the death of her beloved husband, but this - burying the grandson whom she loved but everyone else hated - was undoubtedly the hardest moment of her life.

"I'm sorry, Joseph," she whispered. "I'm sorry your momma and daddy didn't do a better job with you. I'm sorry I didn't do a better job with your daddy." June choked a little from her tears. "I'm sorry you felt like you had to become what you did."

Reagan White was the third member of the group of women gathered to watch as a backhoe now dumped dirt into the hole that held Dr. Carlson's remains. She had to obtain special permission from her doctors to leave the hospital, but it was worth it to be here. The irony of the situation was not lost on the FBI agent, knowing what she now did about how Joseph had disposed of five of his victims. Reagan heard the woman next to her whispering, but could only make out the occasional "Joseph" and "I'm sorry."

She must be family, Reagan surmised. Agent White was surprised any of his relatives were there, especially given the very public way that his surgeon father and socialite mother had disavowed and disowned their only son. *A grandmother, perhaps?* Reagan thought. It didn't really matter who the old woman was, or who the person on the other side of the wheelchair was either - even though Reagan recognized her as Dr. Keri Dupree. It didn't matter who the other women were or why they had gone through the trouble of finding out about the burial and attending it.

Reagan had her own reason, a far less complicated one than her two counterparts: she needed closure. Needed to see, with her own eyes, that Dr. Joseph Isaac Carlson, Jr. was truly dead and buried. He tried to kill her - and nearly succeeded. He *had* succeeded in killing ninety-one people, ninety-two if you included himself, and injuring thirty-five more. But what grated on Reagan more than anything was that he tricked her. Played her for a fool. Agent White knew she would never be able to get rid of the memory of sitting in Carlson's office and asking him questions about the supervirus.

"If it does turn out that there's some mad scientist running around killing people, I want to know about him." Reagan grimaced at the memory of the terrorist doctor's words. *He must have been so proud of himself.*

"Bastard."

Agent White saw the woman beside her turn her head ever-so-slightly when Reagan swore. Before she could open her mouth to apologize, the elderly grandmother said:

"No, dear, it appears you're correct. He was my grandson, and I'll always love him, but you can call him every name in the book if you want to, honey. I understand."

The cemetery's groundskeeper interrupted the women's conversation.

"That's it, ladies. I was told to not leave any kind of headstone or marking, so it's done." He paused, not really knowing what to say. He had never done a burial like this one before. "The gates are already closed for the night; you'll have to come with me so I can let you out."

Keri nodded and stood up a little straighter, preparing to walk back over to her car. The live-in nurse that Joseph Sr. had hired for his mother walked over from their rental car, ready to return the elderly woman back to her Seattle home. Reagan, however, remained still.

"Ma'am, did you hear me?" the groundskeeper asked.

Without taking her eyes off the grave, Reagan replied with a soft "yes." Then: "would you mind giving me a hand? Wheeling myself out here was harder than I thought it would be."

The groundskeeper nodded and took a step in her direction but then stopped. Reagan heard a familiar voice behind her.

"It's alright. I've got it."

She turned her head to the side to see Allen standing a few feet away. He smiled.

"Hi."

The bruises on Reagan's face had healed enough to let her smile back. "Hi yourself."

"You know, when they said I would be working with the Bureau's best field agent, I didn't expect you to be so young. Or a girl."

Reagan tried to laugh but winced, grabbing her ribs in pain. "Shut up and push, Williams."

"As you wish, madam." Allen then spun the wheelchair around on the grass and began to walk Reagan back to his car.

Behind them, the cemetery groundskeeper drove a heavy machine back and forth over the fresh plot of dirt, packing it down just as the buried man had previously done in the national park nearby. Looking over her shoulder, Reagan released a heavy sigh and shook her head.

"It all really does come full circle in the end."

###

Please consider writing a review on Amazon.com!

Sample Chapters: THE CONTAINMENT ZONE

ONE

A seven year old little girl with pigtails and sparkling blue eyes was the first one to say something to Luke Russell about the spots on his face.

"What's that?" young Sophia asked, scrunching up her cheeks and pointing her finger at the nose of the man doing repair work in her school. The weather that September in Shorewood, Minnesota was unseasonably hot, and the school district had sent its in-house electrician over to Minnewashta Elementary to make sure the air conditioning was working properly.

"What's what?" Luke asked, taking a break from work to wipe sweat from his brow.

"Those dots," Sophia replied, pointing again at the man's nose. "The ones all over your face." The little girl's missing front teeth meant that each word was pronounced with a lisp, something the forty-two year old father remembered well from when his own kids were that age.

"I don't know, honey. I don't have any spots, last I checked."

The second grader kept looking at him, intent on figuring out the mystery, until her teacher called her back to the line for recess. "Leave Mr. Russell alone," the woman scolded, smiling sympathetically at him from down the hall. With a population just over 7,000, Shorewood was the kind of town where everybody knew each other. It also didn't hurt that Luke's children still attended the school.

Dots on my face, he thought. *Kids sure do have active imaginations.* Russell forgot about the encounter and went back to work, tweaking and tightening the central air system to keep it running through the rest of the Indian summer. No one else mentioned anything looking amiss about him, but then again Luke didn't talk to anyone else during the rest of his time at the school. After checking in at the front office that morning and eating lunch with his nine year old son LJ, Russell was left alone with his work for the day.

It wasn't until he returned home that afternoon that little Sophia's mention of the dots on his face returned to Luke Russell's mind. After taking a shower to clean up from a sweaty, dirty day at the school, Luke used his towel to wipe the steam off the bathroom mirror. Once clear, he saw that the girl hadn't been imagining things after all. Red dots, about the size of his pinky nail, were scattered all over his face, neck, and the upper part of his chest.

"What the hell?" Russell asked aloud, touching on the spots with his fingers. "That's so weird." Luke's skin didn't itch, and he otherwise felt fine, but the rash looked horrible. *I wonder if I was allergic to something in the air vents at the school*, he thought, continuing to press on the red dots with confusion and surprise. After a few minutes, Luke decided to take a Benadryl and see if that made it any better.

****

At 5:30pm that afternoon, Cindy Russell arrived home from her job as an office receptionist to find her children playing in the yard with other neighborhood kids and her husband napping on the living room couch. It wasn't an uncommon occurrence, especially since the local government often needed Luke to work night shifts to fix electrical problems without disrupting other municipal activities.

Forty-five minutes later, with dinner finished cooking, Cindy called her children inside and walked into the living room to wake up her husband.

"Dinner's ready, babe," she said, touching him on the shoulder and turning on a lamp next to the couch. "Oh my God – Luke! What happened?"

"Huh? What?" he replied, drowsy from his medicine-induced sleep.

"Your face!" his wife said. "You have a rash all over it."

Luke lifted up his t-shirt and looked down, noting to his own dismay that the strange circular dots had spread down to cover his whole chest and the upper level of his ribcage.

"Yeah . . . I dunno. Some little girl at the school noticed it first this afternoon, but I think it's gotten worse since then."

"Does it itch?" Cindy asked, leaning down to get a closer look.

"No, thank goodness. It's weird, right?"

"Very." Cindy continued to stare at her husband with the same look on her face that young Sophia displayed earlier that day. "Have you taken anything for it?"

Luke nodded. "Some Benadryl. That's what made me fall asleep."

"Do you have the rash anywhere else? Does anything else hurt or feel funny?"

"What's going on?" asked Madison, the Russells' eleven year old daughter. She had finished washing up after playing and joined her parents in the living room. "Ewww! Dad! Yuck!"

"What?" LJ said, the little boy running in to see what cool thing was making his sister upset.

"Both of you go into the kitchen," their mother ordered, shooing the two children away from their father. "Go eat your dinner before it gets cold."

"But – "

"Go," Luke said, ending any argument before it began.

After Madison and LJ left the room, Luke finally addressed his wife's question. "I have a pounding headache," he said. "And my joints hurt. It honestly feels like the flu, honey, except for the rash part."

"Hmm . . . well, you stay here and rest. Are you hungry? I'll bring you a plate. We'll check your temperature, and I'll see if I have any flu medicine left over from last year."

TWO

Later that night, with her two children fed and put to bed and her sick husband still sprawled out on the couch drifting in and out of sleep, Cindy Russell began cleaning the kitchen, making school lunches, and taking care of the million other little household tasks that, if she didn't do them, would never be done.

Multi-tasking as always, Cindy also pulled out her iPhone and opened her Facebook app. "HELP!" she typed, "DOES ANYONE KNOW WHAT THIS IS?" She then added a picture of her husband's polka-dotted face and chest. "LUKE ALREADY HAD CHICKENPOX SO I KNOW IT'S NOT THAT," Cindy continued typing. "HE ALSO HAS A FEVER, HEADACHE, AND JOINT PAIN. HAS ANYONE ELSE HAD THIS BEFORE? PLEASE HELP!"

Seven likes and twenty-four comments later, the office receptionist still didn't have any good answers. Her co-worker noted that it was possible to get chickenpox more than once, but Cindy replied that the spots didn't itch. A neighbor whose daughter was a nurse suggested maybe eczema, but Luke's rash didn't match the pictures of eczema that Cindy saw online. Her aunt Louise, writing from her nursing home in Boise, said it reminded her of people she knew as a kid who got Measles. "WE DON'T HAVE MEASLES IN THE US ANYMORE, AUNT LOUISE," the younger woman wrote back incorrectly. "PLUS, LUKE HAD THE MMR VACCINE WHEN HE WAS A KID." Four people liked that comment.

Putting her iPhone down on the kitchen counter, Cindy sighed and looked over at her husband who was lying on the couch, his dinner plate resting untouched on his chest. "You're just going to have to go to the doctor, honey," Mrs. Russell said. The rash had continued to spread from Luke's face to his torso and now was beginning to creep onto his arms and legs. "I'll call them first thing in the morning to make an appointment."

****

Luke Russell's primary care doctor at Park Nicollet Clinic in their hometown of Shorewood took one look at his rash, vital signs, and blood test results and sent him straight to the hospital. "The fever is interfering with your body's normal operations," Dr. Norris told him. "And the blood tests show some signs of early organ function deterioration. I won't sugar coat it, Luke," he added, looking his childhood friend in the eye. "It doesn't look good at all. I mean it, buddy. Don't pass go; don't collect two hundred dollars. Get to the hospital as soon as you can."

While Shorewood had no hospital of its own, there were two both within twenty miles of the town. Dr. Norris sent Luke to Ridgeview Medical Center in Waconia, Minnesota, calling ahead to let them know that his patient needed to be admitted and examined as soon as he arrived. Cindy accompanied her husband to the hospital after making arrangements for a neighbor to watch the Russell kids after school.

As instructed, the team at the 105-bed Ridgeview Medical Center was ready and waiting for their newest patient. Luke and Cindy were escorted past everyone in the Emergency Room and into the treatment area. "If you could just wait here," an orderly told Mrs. Russell, "we'll take him back and get him admitted. Once he has a room, we'll come get you."

Three hours later, Cindy was finally led back through the hospital and reunited with her husband. An IV drip was hanging beside Luke's bed to help keep him hydrated, and he had bruising around his veins from multiple rounds of drawing blood. Just as his wife sat down beside the hospital bed and took Luke's hand in her own, a doctor walked into the room.

"Oh, no, don't get up, ma'am," the handsome, late-thirty-something man said. "You're fine there were you are." He smiled at the Russells as a form of introduction, and Cindy liked him immediately.

"I'm Dr. Keith Craig," he continued. "I'm an attending physician here at Ridgeview, and Mr. Russell, sir, I'm going to be taking care of you."

A weakened, pale Luke slowly closed and reopened his eyes as acknowledgement.

Walking over to check his patient's monitors, Dr. Craig asked: "Mr. Russell, is it alright if I discuss your condition in front of your wife?"

When Luke nodded yes, the doctor said: "we've taken the test results that your primary care physician sent us and run a number of our own diagnostic inquiries. Unfortunately, we're still coming up empty. While I'm obviously interested in finding out what's causing the rash and the other symptoms, my first concern right now is getting that fever down."

"So what does that mean?" Cindy asked.

"It means we're going to give him some more ibuprofen and try a few more things, including putting some cooling blankets on your husband to try to lower his body temperature. In the meantime, can you tell me of any unusual things Mr. Russell may have eaten or otherwise been exposed to recently?"

Cindy let out a deep breath and shook her head. "No, not that I can think of."

"Does he have any allergies that aren't noted on his file?"

"No."

"Anything else out of the ordinary happen in the last couple of days?"

"The lake," Luke whispered.

"The lake?"

"Oh yeah," his wife said. "He fell in the lake on Saturday while he was fishing. That's not really something weird or anything like that, though."

"This is Lake Minnetonka we're talking about?" Mrs. Russell nodded her head in the affirmative. Dr. Craig was inclined to agree with his patient's wife that the unplanned swim wasn't important, but he took note of the incident anyway. "Okay, well I'm going to go order up the medicine and cooling blankets as well as some more tests. Someone will be back to check in soon."

Like what you're reading? The rest of *The Containment Zone* is available for purchase on Amazon.com!

ABOUT THE AUTHOR

Danielle knew she was born to be a writer at age four when she entertained an entire emergency room with the - false - story of how she was adopted. *The Enemy Within* is Danielle's third novel. She is a graduate of Georgetown University (Go Hoyas!) and Harvard Law School. Danielle lives in Georgia with her chocolate lab, Gus.

Please consider writing a review online at Amazon.com!

Find out more about Danielle's other books at her website:
www.daniellesingleton.com.

Made in the USA
Columbia, SC
15 June 2020